An esoteric message on a simple headstone
leads a young man to discover...

A RICH MAN'S
SECRET

(The Key to Wealth & Wisdom Lies Just *Beyond* Your Thoughts)

*W*hen he saw the headstone, he sensed it had special meaning, a message that he was meant to learn. He knew no more than that. Something impelled him to learn more about who was in this grave.

*T*he rich man knew he needn't leave a step-by-step "treasure" map to his secret parchment: The "steps" leading to his hidden treasure were invisible and existed beyond physical evidence—outside anyone's mind. They were there, awaiting whomever would leave his or her mechanical thinking behind and take the step of faith required to enter the unknown. These directions—this road map—can't be misplaced and cannot fade. They're permanent—beyond time!

About the Author

Ken Roberts has had an incredible career. Like so many of us, he spent years studying self-help guides, moving from job to job, and worrying about how to achieve personal and professional success. Like so many of us, he thought he knew the answer, but his schemes fizzled. And then Ken discovered the inner principle that you too will learn in *A Rich Man's Secret*. His book is unique, with none of the recycled and fruitless adages that you find crowding the self-help shelves. Ken Roberts is an American "everyman" who found success. Today, his philosophical and financial guidance has reached over 200,000 subscribers in 86 countries. These people also seek a better life, and find in Ken Roberts a combination of that profound folk wisdom, savvy monetary strategy, and friendly help that comes with the discovery of the surprising principle revealed in this novel.

To Write to the Author

If you wish to contact the author or would like more information about this book, please write to the author in care of Llewellyn Worldwide, and we will forward your request. Both the author and publisher appreciate hearing from you and learning of your enjoyment of this book. Llewellyn Worldwide cannot guarantee that every letter written to the author will be answered, but all will be forwarded. Please write to:

Ken Roberts
c/o Llewellyn Worldwide
P.O. Box 64383-K580, St. Paul, MN 55164-0383, USA

Please enclose a self-addressed stamped envelope for reply, or $1.00 to cover costs. If outside U.S.A., enclose international postal reply coupon.

Free Catalog From Llewellyn Worldwide

For more than 90 years, Llewellyn has brought its readers knowledge in the fields of metaphysics and human potential. Learn about the newest books in spiritual guidance, natural healing, astrology, occult philosophy, and more. Enjoy book reviews, new age articles, a calendar of events, plus current advertised products and services. To get your free copy of *Llewellyn's New Worlds of Mind and Spirit*, send your name and address to:

Llewellyn's New Words of Mind and Spirit
P.O. Box 64383-K580, St. Paul, MN 55164-0383, USA

A RICH MAN'S SECRET

AN AMAZING FORMULA FOR SUCCESS

Ken Roberts

1995
Llewellyn Publications
St. Paul, Minnesota 55164-0383, U.S.A.

FIRST EDITION
Third Printing, 1995

Cover design: Anne Marie Garrison
Cover art and interior art: Charles Shields
Book design and layout: W design
Editor: Rosemary Wallner
Project coordinator: Jessica Thoreson

Library of Congress Cataloging-in-Publication Data
Roberts, Ken, 1951–
    A rich man's secret : an amazing formula for success / Ken
Roberts.
    p. cm.
    ISBN 1-56718-580-0
    1. Motivation (Psychology)—Fiction. 2. Success—Fiction.
I. Title.
PS3568.023878R5   1995
813' .54—dc20   95-6490
                                                          CIP

Llewellyn Publications
A Division of Llewellyn Worldwide, Ltd.
P.O. Box 64383, St. Paul, MN 55164-0383

ACKNOWLEDGMENTS

My special thanks to Guy Finley, whose inspiration, insight, and encouragement helped bring *A Rich Man's Secret* to light. Each of his books is a touchstone you will remember and refer to often.

BOOKS BY GUY FINLEY:
Available from Llewellyn Publications:
The Secret Way of Wonder
The Secret of Letting Go
Como Triunfar Sobre La Ansiedad y Los Problemas
Freedom from the Ties that Bind
Designing Your Own Destiny

Lives of great men all remind us

We can make our lives sublime,

And, departing, leave behind us

Footprints on the sands of time;

Footprints that perhaps another,

Sailing o'er life's solemn main,

A forlorn and shipwrecked brother,

Seeing, shall take heart again.

CHAPTER 1

What is it? What is it I need to know? Victor asked himself as he reached to answer the phone.

"Hello, Victor!" said his wife, Christine. "My office just called. I qualified for that big sales contest we were having!"

Victor held the phone tightly to his ear and began to cry. *Where are all these tears coming from? What's going on?* The tears scared him. He could remember crying as a little kid, but never past grade school. *Pull yourself together*, he thought. *Don't upset Christine.*

"That's great, honey. What's the prize?" Victor asked, trying to sound upbeat.

"Since I made those last two listings, we get to go with the others on a secret getaway for a whole week," Christine explained.

"A secret?" asked Victor, "A secret where?"

"Well, it's a secret," laughed Christine.

Victor didn't understand. "You mean we're going to drive to your office, get on a bus, and it's going to take us someplace—and we don't know where?"

"No," said Christine, "We're going to fly there!"

"Fly?" exclaimed Victor.

"Yes; the bus will bring us to LAX from the office and we'll board a plane for I don't know where. When we land, we'll get on a smaller plane and it will take us to our secret destination. Isn't that romantic?" Christine giggled.

"You mean you don't have a clue as to where we're going?" asked Victor.

"No, we were only told what I just told you. No one has an inkling as to where we're going," explained Christine.

Well, where could it be? Victor wondered. *What is it…what am I doing wrong? Do I think differently from everyone else? What is it I need to know, and how do I find it?* With promises that they'd talk about the trip later, Victor Truman said good-bye to his wife, hung up the phone, and began searching the want ads again, wondering if he would ever find his Right Place.

Ever since high school Victor knew he wasn't cut out to follow the path his friends planned on. Working for a big company and applying for a nine-to-five job were just foreign to him. He dreaded the thought; it simply wasn't of his nature, like oil and water.

I'm not lazy, he thought, *in fact, I feel like a powerful transmitter—with no outlet to plug into. But what am I supposed to do? My dad says I just haven't found my Right Place. I wonder if there really is such a thing for me.*

Victor thought back on all he had tried. While still in high school, he performed magic at parties and church groups. After graduating, he landed a seasonal job at Universal Studios, the motion picture complex. That ended when the summer crowds went home, so he enrolled at a local college and worked part-time at a clerical job.

He recalled sitting in the college parking lot before his first class in the morning, staring at his textbooks. There was something so foreboding about them; like a fly in a bowl of soup, he just didn't belong. After his first semester, Victor made the Dean's list—of scholastic probation. He wasn't slow, merely out-of-place, like a dog-lover at a cat show.

Victor's search continued: self-help books, seminars, self-employment, unemployment, meditation, relaxation regimens, career counseling, therapy...each one costing more than the last. Still he remained unfulfilled; and he wasn't making ends meet financially either.

Now thirty, married, and the father of a son and daughter, Victor lived with constant conflict: torn between "heaven and earth"—his earthly responsibilities of supporting a family and the still, small Voice telling him there is Something more, that his Right Place did exist. He was exhausted from the search. It wasn't an issue with him of whether to keep on trying, his concern was how much longer he could hold out.

Deep within, Victor felt impelled to teach. *How do you like that!* he laughed to himself. *I can't get my own life straightened out, but something tells me to teach!* What would he teach, anyway—how to search for (but not find) your happiness?

Although it shook his pride as a father and husband, Christine had obtained her real estate license and had gone to work selling homes in Southern California. Victor began selling life insurance, so both his and Christine's schedules were somewhat flexible. They alternated and helped one another deliver and pick up their two children from a local preschool.

The real estate brokerage Christine chose to apply with was a small firm with offices in a well-to-do area in the San Fernando Valley. Christine became one of this close-knit group of agents.

The brokerage was owned by a husband-and-wife team. Les was a motivator, and did it well. Although he never enjoyed much success as a salesman on his own, his office consistently ranked near the top of sales comparison charts of other agents in the area. Ann was a sweet, mild woman with a keen business sense who ran the day-to-day operation of the office.

Les was a convivial man and that was the atmosphere in the office. "Work together, play together" was his motto. At least once a month he arranged a special outing. All the agents and their spouses met at the office and boarded a chartered bus that would take them to a special restaurant or event. Victor loved—and dreaded—these outings.

He looked forward to the camaraderie, to being with Christine's fellow agents and their husbands and wives. Most of them were very successful in their own work or business and he enjoyed being with them in casual, social surroundings. He was ever-hoping to learn the reasons for their seeming success. This also brought up the inevitable comparison— between himself and them.

They were well on the way, already enjoying what he strove for: big houses, custom furnishings, expensive automobiles, tax shelters, private schools for their children, excess cash and the free time to spend it.

Once on an office junket to Palm Springs, the group had gathered in the hotel lounge to plan the afternoon activity. Some of the group wanted to stay at the hotel and play tennis; the others wanted to go shopping. Victor felt a pang when one of the women said, "My husband makes more than enough money, why shouldn't I go spend some of it?" If only he could tell Christine to go out and spend what she wanted. Heaven knows she deserves it.

Raising two children, taking care of a husband who doesn't know his Right Place, trying to catch up on credit card debt, working as a real estate agent...all this in the confines of a rented 800-square-foot house. Yet Christine did it all with grace, style, and an ever-present smile on her face, encouraging Victor in whatever his latest plan happened to be.

At home later that night, a tremendous wave of failure and frustration washed over Victor. It filled him all at once with feelings of guilt, anger, remorse, jealousy, hopelessness, and self-pity.

"I can't go," he told his wife. "How can I go when we have so many bills to pay, not to mention all that we need when and if they ever do get paid?" The thought of everything overwhelmed him, and he slumped down onto the couch.

"Oh, Victor..." Christine looked down at him with such sadness, but she knew she'd better try to pull him out of this state before he definitely made his mind up to not go. "...you *have* to go. I won't have any fun without you. Besides, you're always the one who has the best time of all. Everyone likes you, Victor; we'll *all* miss you."

Victor looked at Christine's cute, pouty face and smiled, still feeling guilty. She was so petite and sweet. He felt like her third child rather than the supposed head of the household.

Head of the household, he thought. *Sure! Poor Christine holds this family together* and *makes more money than I do!*

"No, hon, I just can't go. It'd probably do you good to not have me around your neck for awhile anyway. You just go and I'll try to close some sales while you're gone."

Christine's face dropped, and she went to the kitchen to start dinner. The phone rang and she answered it. "Oh, hi, Les…yes, he's here. Just a minute." Victor looked up and saw Christine holding the phone out.

"Hello?" said Victor, taking the phone.

"Hello, Victor. How's it goin'?"

Victor was surprised; Les had never called specifically for him before. "Fine, Les. How are you?"

"Great, Victor, just great. Listen, did Christine tell you? I'm very excited about this mystery trip we're taking; I think it's really going to do you a lot of good."

"Why do you say so, Les?"

"Oh, I don't know. You've been on my mind and I think this trip is going to be good for you, too."

"Well, thanks, Les. It's nice of you to call."

"Atta boy, Victor. Keep on keepin' on!" Les sounded like Victor's father.

"Thanks…bye."

"That was different. What did he want?" Christine was smiling, eyes wide.

"Yes, it was different. Les never did that before. Said he'd been thinking about me lately, and that the secret trip was going to be good for me." Victor was looking out the window, wondering what Les' words really meant.

"Then…you're going?" Christine asked in a rising voice, anticipating a yes answer.

Victor brought his gaze back to Christine. She could tell he was still trapped in thoughts of guilt and gloom. "We'll see," he said, walking out of the kitchen.

At least there's some hope, Christine considered. She called after him: "I love you, Victor."

Victor was up well before the children and Christine the next day. He was watching the morning show when Christine came and snuggled under the blanket with him on the couch.

"What time did you get up?" She kissed him on the cheek.

"Five-thirty," Victor said, just as surprised saying it as Christine was to hear it.

"Five-thirty? What's going on?" she said, teasingly.

"I don't know. I even tried to go back to sleep, but I had to get up."

"Who's this?" Christine asked, looking at a well-dressed woman on the television.

"Some kind of business psychologist," Victor answered.

"...and," continued the psychologist, "not only are business trips where the spouse goes along *more* productive than the 'leave-the-spouse-at-home' jaunts that corporations are infamous for, but the children of these marriages benefit greatly as well."

"Really? How so?" asked the show's host.

"It's *good* for children to be away from both parents at times. Children need vacations from their parents just as much as parents need time away from their children."

Christine looked at Victor, who couldn't help but smile.

"Then that settles it?" she pronounced, slapping him on the knee.

"Okay. The kids win, and get a vacation from *both* of us." Victor leaned over to kiss Christine as she hugged him around the neck.

CHAPTER 2

The big morning came. Victor and Christine were all packed, the car was loaded, and they were off to her office. Although they were given general instructions—how to dress for the climate they would be in, and what types of activities would be available, they still had no idea where it was they were bound for.

Enthusiasm was high as the agents and their spouses greeted their traveling companions and transferred luggage from their cars to the waiting bus, its engine running and air conditioner going. Soon, they were off on the forty-minute trip to Los Angeles International Airport.

The conversations and commotion weren't as diverse as usual. This trip prompted one main topic: Where were they headed? Speculation ran up and down the rows of seats. They didn't need passports for this journey, so that limited the guessing—but only slightly. Everyone on the bus had his or her own theory and eagerly explained the reasons behind it. Christine secretly hoped they were bound for Hawaii.

Victor was smiling, but—as always—comparing himself to the other husbands. The other men were well-traveled, and had all the latest in sports gear, clothes, even luggage. He listened to them name places they had been that he had never even heard of. There was one obvious fact that Victor was aware of, but he usually pushed aside in his comparisons: Although the others had more money and seemingly solid occupations, they weren't happy—not really. Their smiles and talk were convincing on the surface, but just beneath the polished veneer Victor could see the same fears and anxieties he had. The better he had come to know these people, the more he had noticed this.

The others managed to pay the bills and keep up on the latest food, fashion, and furnishings, so they were comfortable in their ruts. Victor wasn't, so he searched harder. That was the only difference.

After devouring the greater part of the self-help and success books on bookstore shelves, he knew from himself that they all missed the mark somehow. What was this mark, this elusive Something, that needed to be understood? All the books, strategies, methods, and techniques that Victor had studied and pursued claimed authority based on one of only two premises: One, that we can control outside events, or two, that we should work to control and change our thoughts.

Victor had already concluded that attempting to control outside events is futile because, if we can indeed control outside events, with what do we control them? Any control, if it were possible, would have to come from something we do, and anything we do is determined by our thoughts. So this conclusion leads to the second genre of self-help/success books: that we can control our thoughts.

But can we? We know something is awry in our thinking—with our thoughts—or we wouldn't try to change them!

Isn't something inherently wrong with this? What is the source of these negative, harmful thoughts? Nothing I've ever read or tried answers this, which must be the reason why the "positive-this," *"subconscious-that," and "hidden such 'n' so" don't work,* Victor reasoned. *So what is the secret?*

"Oh, look! We're here!" Christine was leaning forward in her seat and touching the tinted window with her finger. Conversations got louder as the bus pulled up to the domestic airlines terminal and stopped. With a loud blast of air and a grand slap, the big bus door swung open.

In one large, bounding mass, the excited group moved through the electric double doors of the terminal and stopped in line at the metal detectors. A few were detained because of belt buckles, pocket change, and metal sunglass frames.

I wish Christine and I had Rolex watches so big they set off *every bell, light, and siren in this building,* Victor thought to himself, looking down at Christine. She looked like a little girl standing in line, wide-eyed, her big white teeth showing through a smile of anticipation. Just as he was enjoying this vision, feelings of guilt descended again: *You can thank* *Christine for this trip. What's wrong with you? You're the one who* *knows all the success formulas forward and backward, but it's your* *wife who delivers the rewards!*

His feelings really got control of him: *You're just lazy! She's* *got less experience than you do, yet she wins this trip. Why aren't* *you the successful real estate salesman?*

Les and Ann, ever-smiling at the group's guesses of city names being tossed up to them, but never saying a word, led them to departure gate three. As they turned into the waiting area, they all spotted the lettered flight number and destination sign posted at the ticket counter. In unison they said it aloud. Knowing they would take a shuttle flight from there, the guessing now narrowed down to one or two states.

Even though the primary destination was known now, they were hard-put to come up with where a smaller plane might be taking them. The suspense was ever greater now, although the guessing lessened. Knowing more of the puzzle meant they now knew less.

The views below transformed from the dry, sandy, barren deserts of the southwest to green terrain spotted with more and more rivers, lakes, and ponds.

After settling down through layers of thick lazy clouds, the kind not often seen in Southern California, the plane landed and came to rest at the terminal. Although the telescoping walkway from the terminal to their plane was fully enclosed, the outside heat and humidity crept in. As they passed through it and on into the air-conditioned terminal, the air became chilly again.

It was a long walk to the escalators that took them down into the baggage area. With luggage in hand, the smiling group boarded a tram that took them on a short trip to what appeared to be the local commuter airlines terminal.

With the usual rubber-band-engine and bird-strikes-from-the-rear jokes, they checked their bags at the one-man counter, passed through what looked to be a makeshift metal detector, and walked across the tarmac to a small twin-engine airplane. Stepping up on what was more of a stool than a stairway, they entered the cabin, which was twelve rows of two seats each with an aisle down the middle. They had to hunch down to walk the aisle and take their seats. Each seat had a window and a headset tucked into the pouch on the back of the seat in front. The cockpit, with a pilot and co-pilot, had a wooden sliding door for separation, but it was never closed during the bumpy flight.

They landed in a farmland area surrounded by large, sprawling blankets of pine trees. There was just one runway at this airport and no control tower.

Here they were, but they still didn't know what that meant. The waiting area in the tiny airline office offered only a vinyl couch and two well-worn chairs, so they meandered outside and congregated under a huge magnolia tree. More confused than ever, they didn't know whether to be elated or disappointed—was this good or bad? The thought that it was all a practical joke crossed their minds, but no one spoke it. Murmurings of "Where are we?" and bits of nervous laughter rose from the gathering as they stood and waited for—they didn't know what. Les and Ann stood in the middle of the group, smiling.

"Look!" someone said, pointing to four vans coming down the long red-clay road. It wasn't raining, but the air was heavy with water, as if it could rain at any moment. The tires of the four vans sent up no dust from the roadway as they approached, alternately appearing and disappearing between the tall trees and high, wild shrubbery lining the access road.

As the vans came closer, into clear view, the group knew this wasn't a joke. Each van was jet black with what looked to be a coat of wax half an inch thick. They looked wet. In small ornate lettering along both sides of each van ran the words Grand Hotel.

Two men jumped from the front seats of each van, walked toward the group, made a shallow bow, and smiled.

"Welcome to the Grand Hotel," their leader said.

Each attendant wore a stiff, trim uniform of black pants with a shiny black silk stripe down the outside of each leg; a stiff, high-collared, snow-white tunic with large brass buttons; and a white cloth-covered helmet with a brim front and rear, similar to those worn by safari hunters in Africa.

As the baggage was loaded into the last van, the group divided itself up into three smaller groups, climbed into the first three vans, and headed back down the red dirt road.

Anticipation was high again; something truly special was just ahead.

The red-clay road made a surprisingly smooth ride. Even though the van's air conditioners provided cool, dry air, the knowledge that it was hot and humid outside was ever present.

The little line of vans turned off the dirt road onto a two-lane asphalt highway. The countryside was gently rolling, basically flat, no hills or mountains, and lush green everywhere. This was almost a tropical climate—all the vegetation was large and abundant. It climbed over fences and up telephone poles with ease. The trees were stout, solid, and shady. This was rich farming country.

Between the areas of natural, thick, jungle-like growth rising some thirty to forty feet high, were flat, smooth-looking acres of crops. There was corn, melons, and soybeans, all planted in perfectly straight rows so long that they'd disappear over one mound and reappear some distance away.

Occasionally, a herd of cows was seen. They passed one herd standing in the end of a shallow pond. The animals huddled under the shade of a giant oak tree, which was dripping with Spanish moss.

Where could they be headed? The skyline included no cities, not even a town. They passed weathered farmhouses with tin-roofed barns and out-buildings. Mostly there were small, single-story, light-colored brick homes set back from the highway a hundred yards or so. Each looked basically the same as the next, with simple, boxy hedges, a magnolia tree or two, and a screened aluminum patio attached. This was a heavenly climate for bugs, which were constantly dotting the van's windshield.

Every so often, the vans passed the impressive gates of large estates. Through most of these imposing arched, brick-shrub-and-wood entrances, the group could trace long meandering driveways, up and down knolls, to where they circled in front of three- and four-story mansions—the kind of "palaces" not often seen, except in movies. These glimpses charged the atmosphere in the vans even more than it already was. The jolt of these occasional sightings made the expectant travelers mentally compare the richness of these passing estates to what lay in store for them at their van's final destination.

Then the little caravan slowed and made a left turn off the highway. There in front of them rose the largest, widest entry arch they had seen so far. Rising up from a cluster of giant camellia bushes, neatly trimmed to form great round mounds, two massive square rough-wood pillars supported a heavy wooden arch, two feet tall, that spanned the entry road. Across the face of the arch in carved gold-leafed letters were the words Grand Hotel. The passengers' eyes widened as the quartet of vans neared the end of its journey.

The scenery inside the gate was not the typical natural, overgrown countryside they had seen on the highway behind them. Here were meticulously cared-for grounds: closely mowed, rolling lawns; tightly trimmed rows of hedges; neatly maintained duck ponds. Although no buildings were in sight yet, evidence of an exclusive resort was apparent. Now they could see part of a golf course several hundred yards off to the right. Its lighter, finer color and texture was speckled with golfers in their brightly colored outfits. Here and there could be seen little electric Grand Hotel maintenance carts with khaki-uniformed drivers.

And there now, just off to the left: a glimpse of wood-and-brick buildings among scores of oak trees. The oaks here looked so different: each one was laced with fragile gray and green Spanish moss that dropped down from strong, thick, outstretched branches.

Expectations were higher than ever now as the vans pulled up and stopped under a wide, arched, ivy-covered brick porte cochere, the Grand Hotel's main entryway.

When the van doors opened, the heat and humidity rushed in. It felt tropical. Victor and Christine moved along with the others through the overly tall double oak doors that two attendants held open, and then into the Grand Hotel.

The lobby rose two stories, with a second-story balcony encircling it. A four-sided rock fireplace was the centerpiece and three hallways opened into this central area. All the furnishings were antique. Except for the telephones and aluminum luggage carts the bellhops pushed along, they could have been standing in the mid-nineteenth century.

The manager greeted Les and welcomed the entourage. He called out each traveler's name and motioned to the next in a line of bellhops that had quietly formed since the group arrived. When their name was called, Victor and Christine followed their guide down the second long hallway from the fireplace.

The hotel was old but richly elegant. The hallway had a rather low enameled wood ceiling and dark wood walls. Old electric-lantern lamps mounted along the walls provided just enough light to navigate by. Dimly lit old framed photographs on the walls revealed the Grand Hotel's history. Victor had to step to the middle of the hallway when they passed occasional small antique tables and chairs placed along the walls of this narrow passageway.

Christine was grinning wider and wider with each step as she anticipated the elegance that was sure to meet them when their room's door was opened.

Slightly more than halfway down the long hall, the bell-hop stopped and faced the door to his left. One-two-three, in small gold numbers. He inserted the key in the lock, slowly pushed the door open, and motioned with his hand and a smile for Victor and Christine to enter their new quarters. Christine was visibly impressed.

"Oh, goodness," she sighed, "it's *exquisite!*"

As much as Christine was elated in these opulent surroundings, Victor was equally depressed. All the usual negative thoughts tormented him: *Remember, it's Christine's doing that you're even here, you loser. You'll never be able to afford anything like this. You don't belong in such plush surroundings—you just don't fit in in a place like this. If you'd quit trying to find your Right Place, maybe you'd make a little progress—that's just an excuse you use because you're too scared and lazy to go get a real job; Christine deserves a lot better than you, that's for sure!*

It was difficult for Victor to look pleased and surprised with all this turmoil and brutality going on in his head.

The group met for dinner that evening in the main dining room, and those thoughts were still working him over:

Everyone's dressed nicer than you. You look so out-of-place. Everyone else is at ease, but you look so stiff and uncomfortable.

As they were finishing their meal, the others began planning the next day's activities. Some would play tennis, a few wanted to sun by the pool, two were going horseback riding, and, as always, several of the women started in about shopping. Victor watched Christine's face, but she didn't even flinch as he expected she should, knowing they didn't have extra money for unnecessary shopping. She spoke of taking a walk and catching up on a book she and some of the other women were reading.

Victor was being bruised by defeating thoughts again, but this time he wondered: *Do the others think like I do, and will I finally feel good about myself once I gain a certain amount of success? How much money and success will do it?*

Nothing the others planned to do the following day interested Victor, so he agreed—much to his own surprise—to go golfing, of all things, with several of the others. He hadn't played much golf and wouldn't make a decent partner, so he suggested that they not count him in as a golfer—just a spectator. He never could understand how businessmen played so much golf—it took a full half-day: *How did they ever get any work done? Maybe some of their success will rub off on you*, his thoughts told him.

Later, as she slipped between the cool, stiff sheets of their king-size bed, Christine said, "I can't believe how quickly you agreed to go golfing tomorrow." Victor chuckled. "I was surprised, too. But you know how part of the golf course came into view as we were driving in here today? All of a sudden, I got this urge to get out on it. Not to golf, but just to enjoy the peace and stillness of it." Victor's eyes trailed off. "So when I heard the words 'golf course' tonight, the word 'yes' just sort of popped out of my mouth."

"Well, I'm so glad you came; I wouldn't have had as much fun without you here. Wasn't dinner delightful? And the china, silverware, lace tablecloths, and napkins were just so delicate and refined...I'm so happy about being here, Victor." Christine kissed him goodnight and tucked the bedding up under her chin, ready for sleep.

Victor looked over and realized that his wife was delicate and refined, too, and those were qualities that he loved most about her. He looked onto her sweet, contented face and leaned down to kiss her nose. *How very fortunate I am*, he thought as he turned under the covers to go to sleep. It wasn't long before the thoughts started at him again: *She should leave you, Victor. If it weren't for her own hard work, she'd never experience the good things in life like this trip; you're sure never going to make it. You're just a millstone around her neck.*

CHAPTER 3

$\mathcal{V}$ictor met his golfing companions the next morning in the hotel's less formal—though still very impressive—breakfast area. Out through tall glass-and-oak double doors across from the fireplace, visitors stepped down into a large—at least thirty yards across—octagonal glass-walled room. A grove of mighty, old oak trees surrounded and overhung every side of the room, so views from it were framed through the oaks. It was all so clean and green outside: the golf course, gardens, walkways, lawns, and natural woodsy stands of pines, oaks, and shrubs in which the Grand Hotel was situated.

In the middle of this room was a large rectangle formed of long serving tables draped with white starched tablecloths. The display was one of the largest breakfast buffets Victor had ever seen. The tables were laden with every kind of egg dish, fish, and a variety of breakfast meats, as well as fresh fruit platters, assorted baked breads and rolls, pancakes, waffles, crepes, and blintzes. If you didn't see what you wanted, one of the four chefs attending from inside this rectangle of food would make it.

Victor loaded his plate and sat down with the other men. Around these people, he listened more than he talked. They all were well acquainted now, having seen each other usually

21

once a month for over a year. They spoke fairly frankly and Victor often felt that there was much he could learn from knowing them. But he never knew what key questions he should ask. The more he was with them, however, the less certain he was that they even knew any "secrets to success."

The more he observed them in these informal situations, the more he began to see little chinks in their armor. One of the men, for instance, was definitely an alcoholic. Victor never saw him falling-down drunk, but he also rarely saw him without a drink in his hand. Victor had asked Christine if she knew how this man's marriage was going. Christine had answered that the man's wife was nearing the end of her tolerance for his drinking. Another of these men represented a Japanese electronics firm that had been king of the hill for two years running in the video game market. He was raking in the money, but also spending it furiously. The last few months, however, he hadn't been so vocal about the health of his business. Victor asked him this morning how sales were going and learned that bad management had severely hurt the firm. This stumble had allowed the competition to not only catch up, but to also significantly surpass the company he represented, so the future was glum. If the company made a comeback at all, the man said, it would be limping for a long while.

As far as Victor could tell, the most well-rounded and successful man in the group was Ray. Ray's wife, Marion, was a good friend to Christine and had helped her along when she first joined the real estate agency. Ray and Marion had two children a few years older than Victor and Christine's. They seemed to be the most happily married couple, and the most stable.

Ray was a self-made man, upper middle-class. He worked hard and ran an executive search firm he and his brother had begun in New York. Ray and Victor got along well, perhaps because they were of the same entrepreneurial bent. Ray always enjoyed Victor's energy and enthusiasm and seemed to understand that Victor was searching for his Right Place and just hadn't discovered it yet. Victor always hoped Ray would have some words of wisdom, or tell him the secret to success that he seemed to possess, but these words never came. Ray, in fact, once offered Victor a position with his company. Ray wanted Victor to act as a kind of motivator for the company sales force who made phone solicitations and presentations. Disappointedly sensing that Ray wasn't withholding some deep secret, Victor did the only thing he felt sure and certain of: Don't work for someone else; work only for yourself. He respectfully declined Ray's offer.

This morning they had eaten a lot and laughed a lot (even though Victor was feeling guilty most of the time for not "earning" this vacation himself), when someone said, "It's tee-off time. Let's hit it!" The golfing group rose and headed for the clubhouse.

Victor had no desire to golf, so he repeated his offer to act as a spectator. "I'll be someone's caddie, or chauffeur one of the golf carts," he said. Actually, driving one of the modern electric carts looked like it would be fun.

After doing whatever golfers do (to Victor, it seemed like so much effort, motion, and expense for not much benefit), the two foursomes and Victor walked out to the cart area, loaded the bags of clubs, and scooted out to the first tee.

It was a gorgeous morning: The sun was still below the tops of the trees and sunlight streamed through their leaves and branches. Dew covered everything. Big loping clouds, some quite low, seemed to dampen the atmosphere. Victor thought the others were talking too much and disturbing the hush that they were entering. It was cool and pleasant, but you could feel the heat and humidity building, waiting to descend at just the right moment. It would be hot and muggy after a while, but for now, this was a calm and blissful setting.

Victor enjoyed driving the cart and tried to be as helpful to the others as he could. He fetched clubs, replaced divots, wiped the wet grass off golf balls, and was quite enjoying his day "golfing."

The sun was hotter and higher now, nearly overhead. And it was humid. The birds seemed to fly a little slower, and the lush greenery surrounding the fairways drooped a bit under the weight of the air. You always knew where the sun was—you could feel its heat. Warm air rose in twisting ethereal ribbons from the lawn.

"Darn!" exclaimed one of the golfers. Victor looked up just in time to watch a golf ball drop and disappear into the woods next to the fairway.

Before he knew it, Victor blurted out, "I'll find it!" He left the cart and walked over to where the golf course met the woods, probably thirty or forty yards from where the ball landed. The woods consisted of rather thin pine trees, growing densely together. One shot up every three or four feet. Victor could barely see their bases because thick bushes covered the floor of the woods. It looked fairly solid, and Victor was now doubting that he could enter these woods to retrieve the ball at all. He walked along this living wall of woods a ways, looking for a clearing.

"You better get another ball," he called toward the others, "this may take awhile."

"Let it go," someone cried, but Victor was looking forward to this now—"golfing" was getting a little boring.

"I'm gonna find it. You go on and I'll catch up."

With that, Victor was on his own, all alone at the edge of another world. Everything about the golf course—even its ponds—was obviously man-made: the lawn was too perfect, impeccably cut and cared for; the ponds were probably filtered, even their edges were clipped and trimmed; the sand traps, too, were raked, shaped, and smoothed to perfection.

The woods were so quiet. Even the bird calls were muted in this naturally soundproofed place. A heavy, full smell of pine, brush, and moist, decaying leaves and pine needles made Victor breathe deeply to take it all in. He kept looking for an entrance, then found a passable "doorway" to duck through.

Victor smiled as he emerged from this natural tunnel. Standing upright, he stretched his hands overhead and sighed. It was much like a cathedral inside these woods. *This must be the true meaning of the word sanctuary,* he thought, as he walked deeper and deeper into this special new place.

The ground was so deeply padded; it was like stepping on a natural mattress of undergrowth. With each step, Victor sprung slightly with a rustling sound. He looked around to where he thought the ball probably fell, but then he paused.

"I don't want to chase some golf ball," he whispered, "I want to stay in these woods." As soon as he spoke these words, Victor felt a peace wash over him from head to toe. It felt so good, so calm, something new that he never experienced before. A warm, tingling glow filled his face, scalp, and ears. Victor smiled and asked out loud, "What is this?" He closed his eyes, inhaled deeply, and savored this new, rich sensation. After a few moments, he slowly opened his eyes, hoping he wouldn't shatter this delicate moment in which he was immersed. Without thinking, he gingerly turned in the direction opposite of where the golf ball might have landed and took a cautious step forward, trying not to disturb the calmness that had descended. The golf ball had no meaning now.

A dozen strides later, he spotted a clearing some fifty or sixty feet away, surrounded by low, free-growing shrubbery against a very old split-rail fence. He ventured toward the fenced area.

Stepping over the fence through a hole in the shrubbery, he was standing...yes, it was true...in a cemetery.

This was an old cemetery. Victor read some of the dates carved in the headstones: Born 1814, Died 1868; 1827-1901. There was one, 1803-1819. What had he found here? The grass all around was scraggly and gave way to dirt in many places, but it was mowed. The entire grounds consisted of a rectangle about two hundred feet long and a hundred feet wide, cleared out of the woods.

Looking across the cemetery, Victor saw the main entrance: double six- or seven-foot high gates made of swirling, ornate wrought iron. One gate had settled over time, so it didn't quite meet its twin that was partially ajar. Victor could see that there was no lock as he walked toward it. He pushed against the gate that was slightly opened and it creaked.

Just like in a movie, Victor thought, smiling nervously. Outside the cemetery, he now stood on a dirt path that led to the gates from a small paved road passing through the woods nearby. Victor re-entered and looked around this final resting place again.

Most of the headstones looked very old. They were about two-and-a-half feet wide and three feet tall, standing more or less upright from bases made of the same stone. Some were whiter than others, but others were mottled with what Victor guessed to be a kind of black moss. The carvings on their faces were all intact, but the fine black growth made them more difficult to read. These white-but-stained-black stones seemed to be some of the oldest: There was Nicholas Henry Richtor, 1843-1907; Edmund Hinshaw, Native of Virginia, 1821-1872; Henry E. Street, 1841-1889.

In the very center of the cemetery was an area about thirty feet square separated with small square granite posts, eight to ten feet apart. Heavy, dark-metal chains slung between the posts, forming a large yard. A stout, full oak stood in the center. Its sprawling limbs reached out all around and dropped toward the ground, one nearly touching a headstone beneath it. Fragile moss dripped from its mighty limbs.

"This could be a very eerie place at night," Victor said aloud. The sound of his voice surprised him—he looked around to see if anyone else was there. He also noticed he was walking very slowly and carefully—almost a stalking—as if to not let his presence be known.

The chains and pillars at each end of this yard within the cemetery didn't close: They ended four feet short of each other to form an entryway. Standing just outside these openings in the chain at both ends was an old, stubby cannon. Victor walked to the farther one.

The cannon was made from a deep black metal, but it was not smooth and shiny as Victor thought it should be. Rather, this was a soft-looking metal with small indentations covering it, forming an even pattern all over. The cannon was nine or ten inches in diameter at the rear and tapered down to only about five inches at its "business end." The bore also surprised Victor: It was only slightly more than two inches in diameter. The cannon rested in a granite cradle and didn't seem to be attached except by its sheer weight. Victor pushed against its side as hard as he could, but the cannon didn't roll or budge even a bit.

Looking back across this yard to the twin cannon at the other end, Victor noticed that there were no standing headstones in here. As he looked closer, he saw no markers of any kind at all. Looking back again, he noticed an arched gateway spanning the opening in front of the other cannon. Spelled out in letters six inches high, fabricated from the same wrought iron used to make the slim archway itself, were the words Confederate Dead.

"Wow!" Victor blurted, "This is a Civil War cemetery!" This time, the volume of his outburst surprised him even more, and he looked around again. He had walked right past the Civil War arch but missed seeing it because—he could see now—a low-slung limb from an oak tree covered it from that side. He looked about the Confederate Dead yard again for names and dates but found none. *Must have been a mass grave*, he reasoned as he left this area through the archway.

Scanning the cemetery again, Victor noticed that very few headstones stood alone, that most were part of a "set" surrounded and separated by tiny wrought iron fences just a few inches high. Stepping over one of these "groups" near him, he immediately saw the reason for the little fences: These were all family plots. He stood in front of the Thomas family now. There's John, his wife, Mary, her sister, June. In the row behind was the Revere family.

Victor looked farther across the cemetery and spotted a single grave with a larger-than-usual headstone and its own little rectangular iron fence surrounding it. The closer he drew, the more interesting this grave site became. Why was this one so different? One feature Victor noticed was its proportions: Everything about this grave was slightly larger than the others. The headstone itself, its deeply carved letters and numbers, the short ornate ironwork border, were simply larger than any of those surrounding it—larger than any that Victor had seen at all, for that matter.

Who was this? Victor wondered, *an egomaniac? Perhaps the family was the wealthiest in the area.* No, that wasn't it. Several other graves and markers he had seen in the last few minutes were more ornate—some were gaudy even. No, this wasn't an ego trip, but there had to be some reason why this grave was different.

Victor searched for a clue on the headstone itself: There was an arched row of odd-looking forms from the left edge to the right. *Are they flowers? No; too angular. Hieroglyphics?* Victor didn't think so; hieroglyphics look like small pictures, but these didn't. Beneath the arched line of forms was a skeleton key. That could just be generic decoration of the time, like the angels, harps, and hourglasses he had seen on so many other markers.

Then the name, which was no name, just initials: C. W. *Why just initials?* Victor puzzled. Maybe no one knew his name. Maybe he's a she! Perhaps whoever arranged C. W.'s burial used his or her nickname. The dates, 1852-1933. He—or she—was eighty-one. And the phrase: *Take the first step—no more, no less—and the next will be revealed.*

igated some of the surrounding graves, look-
C. W.'s identity. Without any luck, he
W.'s plot and studied it again. He faced it
saw nothing he might have missed before. He
side of it, looking for something unusual. Then
Victor squatted low and circled C. W.'s grave
from this lower angle looking for additional
Nothing.

standing at the foot, Victor found himself staring at
challenging headstone and those words: *Take the first
more, no less—and the next will be revealed.*

spoke C. W.'s instruction aloud several times. "If I
right now," Victor said, "that would mean stepping for-
ght onto the grave itself! Really? Could this be what
message means? Isn't that sacrilegious? What if someone
?" He looked around the cemetery again very slowly.

Victor lifted his right foot into the air. Hesitating mid-
, he gently set his foot down in the hallowed bed, bringing his left foot up and forward to meet the right. Victor
exhaled aloud and let his weight settle in on both feet. He
breathed a little faster and shallower.

Victor looked down from his new, uncomfortable position; from this steep angle above C. W.'s headstone. There,
clearly displayed in front of him as he looked down, protrud-
ing out from the face of the granite tablet, were letters and
numbers. Yes—there they were! August 4, 1899. Plain as day.

Now what? According to the other dates on the marker,
C. W. had apparently died in 1933, so August 4, 1899, was a
day he or she was alive.

Victor left the cemetery by its main gates, walked down the little dirt path, and out onto the paved road. This road was too narrow to be a main highway, and Victor didn't see any road markings. An occasional car passed, so it seemed to be a public thoroughfare. Victor turned right, as this seemed to be the direction back to the Grand Hotel.

Victor's mind was busy trying to unravel the puzzle he had stepped into—literally. He didn't know what his next step should be, but he was walking briskly, even though the hot, heavy atmosphere made it somewhat laborious.

He had walked what he guessed to be over two miles, maybe closer to three, when a small black Grand Hotel pickup truck pulled up behind him, slowed down, and stopped.

Its driver was a spry little man, perhaps sixty-five years old. Victor thought he looked like one of Santa's elves, only old now.

"Need a lift?"

"Oh, yes, that'd be great," smiled Victor, opening the passenger door. "I'm staying at the Grand Hotel."

"Well, welcome aboard. My name's Pete."

Victor shook the little man's open hand and said, "Thank you very much for stopping. I'm Victor."

"You'd'a had quite a walk ahead of you; this is kind of a roundabout road that takes you a ways from the hotel before it brings you back again to the main road. How'd'ya get out here this far?"

"Well," explained Victor, taking a heavy breath, "I was with some golfing friends of mine and I left them on the sixth fairway, looking for a ball one of 'em hit into the woods..."

The old man chuckled.

"…and it was so pleasant in there, I decided to just leave them and do some exploring."

"It gets pretty thick in some of them woods, did you get all brambled up?" asked Pete.

"No," replied Victor, looking at his legs and arms, "I seemed to do fairly well. I came across an old cemetery in there, so I wasn't in the woods all that much."

"Ah, yes, the old cemetery," the old man recalled. "That's the original town graveyard from a long, long time ago."

"Do you know anything about it?" Victor asked, sitting up a little straighter in his seat.

"No, not much, 'cept that it's a historical site, and when the hotel got that land, they had to keep it up and allow access to it. I was there a couple of times; I think it's special because of those Civil War graves in it."

Victor could tell he wasn't going to learn much more from Pete, so he asked "Where can I find out more about it?"

"Well," Pete thought, tapping his fingers on the stick shift, "why don't you look up ol' Hap. He's been at the hotel longer'n most anyone. I'll bet he knows somethin' about the place."

"Who's Hap?" Victor asked, his eyes widening.

"Hap? Oh, he's the hotel relic. Hap's been around seems like forever. He runs the stables—thinks it's his," Pete chuckled.

They'd been driving ten minutes or so and Victor was glad that Pete had come along when he did. He could see the Grand Hotel main entrance now and considered how yesterday, when he had passed through this entrance, he had no idea that a mystery like he just found in the cemetery would be unfolding. This was something right out of the movies!

"Yep," Pete said, "I haven't taken that road in over a year I'll bet; don't know what made me turn off on it today."

"Well, I'm sure glad you did or I might'a been lost for days!"

Pete pulled under the grand porte cochere and Victor got out.

"Thanks a lot, Pete. It was sure good runnin' into you today! Oh, by the way, do you think Hap's at the stable now?"

"Sure; he's *always* at the stable. Just follow the pathway behind the swimmin' pool. You'll see signs along the way."

With that, Victor raised his hand and gestured good-bye. Pete waved back and drove off around the building.

If what they had told him that morning was accurate, the golf group would be back for lunch in about an hour, so Victor decided to use this time to begin his investigation of C. W.'s esoteric message. He walked through the lobby, past the hotel gift shop, and out to the pool area.

"Where's the path that leads to the stable?" he asked a passing waiter balancing a silver tray of colorful tall drinks on the palm of one hand.

"Right over there, sir," the young man motioned with his head.

"Thanks," smiled Victor, wondering why the waiter called him sir. Do I look that old? No, he probably just said that out of habit. Victor looked around at the sun bathers on the Grand Hotel's handsome black-and-tan chaise lounges. Each lounge had a clip-on smoked plastic sun visor that could be moved in all directions and angles to block out the sun wherever one desired. Some people had the sun visor placed directly in front of their face and read a book held up directly behind it. They looked funny to Victor. He saw three or four ladies from his group, but they either had their eyes closed or were reading, so he silently walked past, across the red tiled pool deck, around the spotlessly clean shuffleboard court, past a colorful flower garden and splashing fountain, to a narrow gravel footpath.

The gravel made a nice crunching sound with each footstep. A few steps along was a small wooden sign with indented white letters: Stable. He followed the path on down a knoll, around a large grove of oak trees, past some small white-and-green buildings he guessed were for maintenance and storage (yet they looked good enough to live in), and on up a slight rise. As he reached the top, the stable appeared.

It was a wooden, barn-shaped building with dark green trim; very neat and tidy looking. To the side of it was a large corral painted bright white. Three handsome, shiny horses stood in the shady areas provided by several huge oak trees that circled the corral. Victor thought this setting would have made a perfect Norman Rockwell painting.

As he approached the building, he noticed a small sign with the now-familiar white lettering: Office. It was attached to the wall next to a Dutch door. The top half was open. Victor walked up and peered in. It looked and smelled just like he imagined a stable right out of the Old West would: hay, leather, wood, and horses. Looking up directly at him from across the barn was a horse standing in a stall. Victor was startled by a nearby voice: "Can I hep ya?"

He didn't quite know where it came from. He then saw what looked like an old lanky cowboy getting up from a wooden chair behind an ancient pigeon-hole roll-top desk. The old man looked weathered, but very friendly.

"I'm looking for Hap," Victor explained.

"You found him. What can I do for ya, partner?"

"Hap, I was on the golf course today and accidentally found the old cemetery in the woods."

Hap nodded. "That used to be a real special spot 'round here, quite a landmark. People used to stroll through it on Sundays after church, then on over to a big meadow that used to be where part of the golf course is now for picnics. It was a right busy place on Sundays: people strollin', kids runnin' and climbin' trees, men pitchin' horseshoes." Hap's eyes trailed off with his voice. He had one of those silly grins on his face, staring off into the hay loft above.

Victor thought twice about continuing: Maybe he would startle the old man. Perhaps embarrass him? Three or four more seconds of uncomfortable silence passed and then Hap snapped awake again.

"Yep, that was a real happy place on Sundays."

"Well, what happened?" Victor wondered aloud.

"The town started movin' more eastward. In my younger days, I helped build a few of those fancy new houses some big shots started puttin' in east of town. They tried to out-do each other: who could build the biggest, fanciest house. Tourists still drive by 'em today—that whole section out past town. Then the hotel owners figured they could buy up a lot of this land here around the original property and make a golf course outta it. Only the few original families that settled these parts were usin' the cemetery to bury their kin, so it kind'a run down and looked shabby mostly. Since the hotel owners wanted as much of the land 'round here as they could gather, they made a deal with the city fathers to maintain the cemetery if they could buy the land on both sides of it."

"Is the cemetery still used?" Victor asked.

"Oh yeah, but only by those families whose relations are already in it," explained Hap. "You'll still see a new grave go in once in awhile. And I see flowers ever so often that come outta there in the hotel's compost heap over yonder."

Victor was delighted with the amount of information Hap knew about the cemetery. "Well, do you know who C. W. might have been?"

Hap looked puzzled and repeated the initials, "C. W.?"

"Yes. There's a headstone in the cemetery, about four feet high," Victor put out a hand to demonstrate four feet up from the floor, "with a fancy wrought iron border around the grave."

Hap scratched his head and wrinkled his face. "Well, I'm sure I musta seen it, but I don't recollect the one you mean."

"There's kind of a message on it," Victor continued, coaxing Hap along, "that says, 'Take the first step....'" Victor leaned toward Hap, eyes wide, hand outstretched, anticipating the answer.

Hap tried to remember, but nothing was there. He raised his eyebrows and shrugged. Victor considered asking Hap about the date—August 4, 1899—that seemed to be the secret C. W.'s posthumous message divulged, but he took a breath and reevaluated: No, Hap hadn't even been born in 1899, and what if this mystery he had stumbled onto actually led to a hidden treasure somewhere? Victor thought the best course of action now was to shrug all these questions off as just idle curiosity so as not to raise any suspicion in Hap.

"Oh, I'm sure it's nothing at all. It just surprised me to find a cemetery out there off the golf course like that. But thanks for your time. It was nice meeting you, Hap."

"No problem," Hap waved his hand, "Come see me when you want to take a ride."

"Thanks, I'll do that. So long." *Good. Hap didn't give the questions about C. W. and his cryptic message a second thought. But now what?*

Victor walked briskly back toward the hotel. The humidity slowed his pace, but he still smiled. What a mystery! He was onto a story here. He couldn't wait to tell Christine all about his unusual morning.

Christine was skeptical, but she saw the expectation in Victor's eyes that she had seen so many times before. This is what she loved about him. "Well, what now, Victor?"

"So far, old C. W.'s instructions proved out: I took that first step and it led to the date—August 4, 1899—hidden in the headstone. That can't be an accident."

"You have all week to solve this mystery." Christine smiled and kissed his cheek.

CHAPTER 4

Victor awoke early and opened the curtains. He had missed sunrise but could tell it had been beautiful. The world outside the window was fresh and green and wet. White billowy clouds filled the sky. The birds were already busy working and playing. A large, plump robin, perched on an oak limb just outside, looked very happy. A tangled piece of yarn dangled from his beak. It looked back and forth several times and then took off to finish its chores.

Victor showered and dressed quickly. He had nothing scheduled today, but the anticipation of solving his mystery compelled him to get out and about. Christine was just awakening. She squinted, yawned, stretched her arms, and smiled a "good morning" at Victor. He patted her knee, kissed her forehead, and left for the dining room.

"I'll meet you at breakfast," he whispered.

The hallway's dark wood, low ceiling, and dim lights made it feel so cozy. The floor creaked occasionally under Victor's feet. He imagined this could be the passageway of a lower deck of an old wooden ship. No one else was in sight.

As Victor crossed through the large circular fireplace room, bright sunlight streamed down from the ring of windows towering above. Victor glanced into the hotel registration area off to the right and noticed a husband and wife and their two children checking out.

The oversized wood-and-glass doors were open to the dining room. Light flooded the room through its glass walls. The oaks outside were especially vibrant and sharp. It was a glorious morning. Victor's eyes searched for familiar faces. He smiled and nodded good morning to several of Christine's fellow agents and their spouses. Then he caught sight of "the gang" sitting at three corner tables of the large room. They were louder than the other diners; Victor could hear their laughter and talking across the many tables. The men were just finishing breakfast and saying their farewells before leaving for the golf course.

"Wanna be my caddie today?" one of the golfers asked.

Victor smiled, "No, thanks."

The women got up to leave, too, and asked about Christine. Victor said she would join him for breakfast soon. He sat down at a table for two and looked out at the new day. He enjoyed the silence.

The birds were especially active this morning. They hopped across the perfectly trimmed lawn and fluttered from branch to branch in the oaks just outside the picture windows of the dining room. Victor's thoughts were as active and animated as the birds: *I wonder what it costs to keep this place up? Must cost thousands of dollars a day for all the caretakers around here. How can people afford to stay here—especially with a family? It must be nice to be able to....*

I wonder if Christine and I will ever have enough money to splurge on a vacation like this? I don't deserve to be here. Everyone in this place can just look at me and see that. Why didn't I just knuckle under, go to college, get good grades, and start climbing that ladder? I'd be on the second rung by now. But what company would I have been working for? I don't even know! I can't even imagine what I'd like to be doing. How's that song go? "Don't fall in love with a dreamer, for he'll always let you down." Poor Christine; what a loser she got stuck with. I wonder if she ever thinks of leaving me? I can't even succeed at marriage....

"Hey, good looking. Mind if I sit down here next to you?"

Victor suddenly remembered where he was and realized how sweet Christine's voice sounded.

"Why, yes, I think that would be quite nice," Victor played along as he rose, pulled out a chair, and gestured for her to sit. *I sure don't know what she sees in me,* he thought.

Christine took a deep breath and looked out at the hotel grounds; the view was inspiring. "Did you order breakfast?"

"No, I just got here. Didn't you see the others leaving on your way in?"

"No, I was wondering where everyone was," Christine commented as she picked up the one-page breakfast menu that looked more like a wine list—fancy type and unpro-nounceable names.

I must have been daydreaming longer that I thought, Victor realized.

"You rarely get up before me—could it be that this isn't really you at all; that I'm sitting at breakfast this morning with Sherlock Holmes instead?"

Victor smiled. *She's so insightful,* he thought. *Of course! C. W., the gravestone, and the mystery!*

"That's right; I've got a real-time mystery to solve. I'm on a mission!"

"What's your next step?" Christine asked.

Victor thought of the message on the headstone: *Take the first step—no more, no less—and the next will be revealed.* "I don't know," confessed Victor.

The waiter came to take their breakfast order. Christine and Victor sat and enjoyed the lush countryside just outside the windows. It was so calm and peaceful and quiet here.

"The Grand Hotel limousine departs in ten minutes." A voice in the reception area outside the dining room broke their reverie. Christine and Victor looked at each other and smiled. Suddenly Victor got up, left the table, and hurried out the dining room doors. He returned moments later and began talking before he sat down: "That limousine goes into town and back three times a day."

"Where's town?" asked Christine.

"I don't know, but I'm taking the one o'clock limo to find out. Wanna go?"

"I can't today. The girls are meeting for lunch and then a game of cards."

"What'd'ya you say we have a nice leisurely breakfast and then go stroll around the gardens awhile?"

"Sounds charming," Christine smiled. "It's just so lovely here, isn't it?"

Victor was the only person waiting in the Grand Hotel lobby at 12:50. It was a quiet day inside the hotel, and out. An airplane could be heard high overhead, but then a few chirping birds drowned out the sound of its engines. Occasionally the hotel's wood roof creaked above. *Must be getting warmer outside*, Victor thought.

"The Grand Hotel limousine departs in ten minutes." The same words he heard at breakfast, but much fainter now. They had to travel from the reception area outside the dining room, around the massive stone fireplaces, and through the lobby to reach him. He hoped there wouldn't suddenly be a rush of tourists flooding down the halls from their rooms to catch the one o'clock limo.

Victor stood with his hands in his pockets, pacing the lobby. He glanced outside through the leaded-glass doors, watching for the limo to arrive. He heard an auto engine approaching and pushed on one of the big double oak doors to wait outside.

A familiar black van with its gold Grand Hotel lettering slowly pulled under the porte cochere and stopped. The driver left the engine running and climbed out. He walked around the front of the van, heading for the lobby, and smiled and nodded at Victor.

"It's a hot one today, isn't it?"

"Yes, it is," said Victor, realizing that he was already feeling damp from the high humidity. "Is this the limo going into town?"

"Yes, sir. Climb on in where it's cool if you like. We'll be leaving in just a couple of minutes," replied the driver as he pushed his way through the big oak doors into the lobby.

Victor heard footsteps on the meandering brick path that ran the length of the hotel. It was more of a tunnel, really: old, thick vines completely concealed the posts and trellis along and over the walkway. Two women talking came nearer and nearer, their hard heels clopping on the bricks and echoing through the vine. It was a pleasant sound.

Victor had already decided he wanted to ride in the front passenger seat so he could ask questions of the driver on the way into town. If these two women were riding, too, he knew they would want to sit in a seat together and continue talking.

One of the lobby doors opened and the driver exited. He stopped, held the door open, and continued to look back into the lobby. A few moments later, a woman with two young children emerged holding their hands.

Victor opened the front passenger door of the van and stepped up to the seat. Feeling the dry, cool air inside, he quickly closed the door and waited.

"Okay, everyone goin' into town?" asked the driver as he opened the van's big side door and helped first the woman with children and then the two talking women up the step and into the van's bench seats.

The van was cooling down quickly again as the passengers watched the driver walk around the van, open his door, and climb in.

As they slowly pulled away down the drive and through the imposing Grand Hotel entry arch, the passengers had settled in: The mother was pointing out the sights to her children and the two women were chattering away as before. They turned onto the highway and were soon traveling along at fifty miles per hour.

The driver was a man in his fifties, Victor guessed, and probably a native of this part of the country. He had those tell-tale deep ruts and furrows in his forehead and neck that Victor had noticed on Pete, Hap, and other hotel staff he saw at the clubhouse and dining room. Maybe the humidity causes it, Victor thought.

"So where's town?" Victor asked, starting up a conversation.

"Oh, it's about thirty minutes off yonder." The driver motioned up the road. It's the county seat, actually."

"What's it known for?" Victor asked.

"Well, used to be a big money center—fancy hotels, restaurants, and banks for the rich Easterners who built big ole mansions here along the river to vacation in. Nowadays, it's mostly retired folks and tourists here."

The countryside was green and moist. Moss dangled from many of the trees. Even wooden fences were spattered with moss and of a rich dark color from being saturated with water. White, yellow, purple, and red wildflowers popped out from tall grass and low bushes on both sides of the highway.

They were just now passing the road Victor recognized to be the back road that led to the cemetery where he had found C. W., or vice versa.

"Where does that road lead?" Victor asked, pretending not to know.

"It runs along the edge of the hotel property a ways. Some of the grounds crews use it," the driver explained.

Victor could tell he wasn't going to learn much from him.

The views from the cool, comfortable van were becoming more interesting: Large white mansions rested a good tenth of a mile back from the road, at the top of long winding driveways that ended in a circle. Most were three stories high with dark-colored roofs. An outside porch encircled many of these homes and had an extra little roof over this perimeter porch. The driver called them rain porches and said they were indigenous to this area of the country. Most of these estates had a guest house, usually behind the main house, and two or three out-buildings scattered about the property. *Probably for water pumps and equipment,* Victor concluded.

They were getting closer to town now; the homes were coming along row after row. They were much smaller than the estates and situated on less acreage.

"Are we there yet?" Victor joked.

"Just about," smiled the driver, "just a couple miles more."

Victor had noticed a wide band of trees off in the distance a while back and guessed it was the path of a river. The snaking green band appeared to cross the road they were on a half mile or so ahead. The road curved out of sight, so Victor waited expectantly to verify his theory. Soon, just ahead of them, was what looked like a huge barn with no front or back walls. It was a covered bridge!

"Look! It's so big!" Victor exclaimed. The women and children in back sat forward to see what Victor was so excited over. They didn't seem impressed at all. Probably because they weren't from Southern California where such structures don't exist. The children asked their mother what all the commotion was about, so she pointed out the landmark to them and explained its function and purpose.

The road took on an uphill slope approaching the covered two-lane bridge and Victor was delighted again: "It's a wooden bridge, too!" he announced as the van clattered across. The driver chuckled at Victor's enthusiasm.

The river below was wide and apparently amply deep. A few small rowboats slid by under the bridge, but Victor focused on a large handsome yacht docked several hundred yards away along the river's edge. It was an elegant old natural-wood boat, not the artificial-looking plastic-and-fiber-glass variety.

"That boat looks like the U.S. presidential yacht," Victor stated, but was really asking the driver for more information.

"That's a real genuine beauty," said the driver, "What a vessel she is. Belongs to the orphanage, always has. I was aboard her once years ago. Yep, a real beauty. Her name's *Coincidental.*"

"*Coincidental?*" Victor asked. "What's that mean?"

"Don't know, but I always remembered it," the driver smiled. "She's always kept in tip-top condition, I hear—ship-shape, I guess you could say." The driver seemed proud of his pun and smiled. Victor smiled with him.

This is too good to be true, Victor thought. He wished Christine were with him now. The van had just crossed the grand old bridge, made a quick right turn at a long row of prim and proper Victorian houses, all painted in bright pastels, and came to rest beneath the largest oak tree Victor had ever seen. The road formed a large circle around the oak and led back out the way they drove in. "End of the line," the driver announced.

Victor sensed that something entirely new awaited him here.

What now? Victor wondered. The van would return to this spot at five o'clock to carry guests back to the Grand Hotel, so he had about three-and-a-half hours to find what he was looking for. But what was that? Victor climbed out of the hotel van and watched it pull away through the heavy, low-slung branches of the giant old oak tree.

Victor turned and faced town. *"Inviting" is the word that describes what I'm seeing*, Victor thought. *And "cozy," and "perfect," and "charming," too. Something about this place just makes you want to drink it all in, to embrace it.*

Victor was standing at one end of a rather short block of small shops and businesses on both sides of the street. Each was a complete little building unto itself—some made of brick, some made of wood, and others of stone, but all abutted each other. *Just like Main Street, Disneyland*, thought Victor. He couldn't help but smile and take in a deep breath.

He began walking down the sidewalk, under the cute tidy awnings and past the flower-filled window boxes of each little shop. He just passed A Stitch in Time, a millinery. Now he was in front of The Time Machine with an antique box camera and black cloth hood displayed with old-fashioned photographs of families, couples, and individual portraits of tourists dressed up in clothing and props of the nineteenth century. He especially liked the photo of a stern-looking father, shotgun across his chest, standing guard next to his three angelic daughters gussied up in ribbons and lace dresses.

Next he passed the U.S. Bank, a stout little brick building with heavy, dark-green felt curtains hanging from thick round brass rings attached to shiny brass curtain rods. Victor looked into the bank and what he saw was right out of an old Western: A thin, bald, mustached man wearing a green visor stood behind the teller bars atop a solid oak counter. Bright red garters around each arm held his sleeves up. He was smiling as he waited on a customer who was the only thing "wrong" with this picture: Her fluorescent orange shorts, purple tank top, black nylon fanny pack, and ugly red-and-blue running shoes spoiled the scene.

Victor turned from the bank's front window and continued his entry into this refreshing other-world. He was nearing the end of this street now, and approached First Avenue that ran perpendicular to Main, the street he was on.

On the corner across the street, a large round clock sat atop an ornate iron pole. Two thin, wrought iron arms jutted out just beneath the clock, and each held a clay pot overflowing with blooming flowers and cascading white and purple alyssum. It was exactly two o'clock.

I have three hours, Victor reminded himself. *But three hours to do what?* Just then, the clanging of a brass bell could be heard not far away. Victor looked around, but couldn't find the source. The clanging got louder. He heard the distinctive sound of a small gasoline engine. "Putt putt," "clang clang," and from around the corner appeared a horseless carriage.

A big smile formed on Victor's face. What a truly pleasant and refreshing surprise this was. That's when it occurred to him: He hadn't seen an automobile since he stepped out of the van! As the shiny carriage passed, Victor read the words "Free Shuttle" painted in guilded lettering on its door. The driver was dressed turn-of-the-century style like the banker, but his passengers stuck out like sore thumbs in their iridescent synthetic fabrics, strap-on pouches, and video cameras. He felt embarrassed to be a tourist, too.

But he wasn't; he was here to solve his mysterious riddle. Victor glanced back at the tall round clock. It was a little after two.

He went over the headstone in his mind. The date: August 4, 1899. What happened on that day here in 1899? Victor was daydreaming. When he came to, his eyes were focused on the corner street signs across First Avenue. There, attached to the street sign post was a small metal sign with green letters: Library. An arrow on the sign pointed farther down First Avenue. *That's it!* Victor almost said aloud. *The library! I'll get a newspaper from August 4, 1899.*

Victor began walking along First Avenue in the direction the arrow pointed. Not knowing how far he would be going, or what side of the street the library was on, Victor was alert. He passed more shops—and more tourists. He heard the motor and bell of the horseless carriage returning. But this time he didn't stop to admire it as it chugged past and made a left turn on Field Street. Where was the library?

All the streets he was passing ended at First Avenue: Main Street, the first he had walked along when the van dropped them off; then he turned left when Main Street ended, where the horseless carriage appeared; he passed Section Street, Field Street, and was now standing at the corner of Watt Street where the touristy part of town apparently ended. Watt Street crossed First Avenue and continued on. Here was the first stop sign Victor had seen in town, and this was a point where street traffic began. A row of five steel posts planted right across First Avenue kept motor vehicles from entering.

Victor still saw no library sign and wondered if someone forgot to post one. He looked up First Avenue and saw a large, red-brick three-story building about three blocks away. He waited for a car to turn left onto Watt Street from First Avenue and continued walking up First toward the building. *Maybe the library's up there,* Victor said to himself, still seeing no further signs. He crossed Second Street, then First Street.

Pausing for two cars to pass along First Street, his head constantly moving so as not to miss a library sign, Victor noticed a very old two-story used-brick building diagonally across the street from where he stood. Small arched windows ran across the second story. The first floor of the building was all brick except for the wood-framed glass front door and a wide picture window next to it. Dark green canvas awnings covered both the door and window.

Large, gold-foil, old-German lettering filled most of the window pane: *Daily Gazette • Published continuously since 1880.* Over a hundred years old. Victor smiled. *I wonder if this is the original building? That's probably the newspaper I'm looking for.* He looked up and kept walking. Park Street was just ahead. *Maybe the library's down there.*

A street encircled the majestic three-story red-brick building that housed the courthouse and government offices. Named Capitol Parkway, it created a contrasting border around the closely trimmed lawn and formal rose gardens leading up to the courthouse. On three sides, stretching out from the building, were parks—very large, old trees sheltering meandering pathways and occasional tables and benches. As he approached the curb to cross Park Street, Victor noticed another library sign attached high on the old-fashioned lamp post. It pointed left, farther down the street.

He turned and walked along Park Street. *This must be close to the way it was in the 1800s,* Victor thought. There was a peace and simplicity that was so compelling. He passed Miller's Inn & Dinner House, a two-story brick building with tall, narrow windows and a stiff, striped awning shading the first floor. The heavy wood bar, brass-and-glass ornaments, and thin wooden chairs looked inviting through the curtained front windows. Next he passed Dr. Sims' Apothecary, a one-story painted-brick structure with bright white wooden trim around its front door and windows. Old ceramic leech jars and thick glass bottles of all colors adorned the twin display windows. Victor wondered whether this was a functional pharmacy or a museum, but he didn't stop to find out; the library awaited.

Continuing past Walker's Mercantile and several unmarked shops and buildings, Victor arrived at the end of Park Street. A solitary two-story wood-framed building stood before him. It could have been a private home but for the little wooden sign posted in the front lawn: Library. A white picket fence bordered the front yard. Victor opened the small gate, strode up the stone walkway, stepped up onto the porch, and entered the front door.

Apparently this hadn't been a private residence after all: inside was just like a library, only smaller. Filling just one large room was everything you'd expect in a library: book shelves, tables and chairs, card files, magazine racks, and copy machine. A stairway rose to the second floor, which Victor assumed was filled with more of the same. Coming through the front door placed one directly in front of the librarian's desk.

"Hello, may I help you?" The librarian was an attractive young woman probably in her early twenties, slender and wholesome-looking with deep brown hair, blushed cheeks, and the most beautiful dark blue eyes Victor ever remembered seeing.

"Yes, thank you," he answered, noticing how nicely conservatively she was dressed: a simple straight navy skirt, pretty white blouse with lace collar, and a thin navy blue ribbon tie formed into a large droopy bow.

"I'm looking for a copy of a newspaper from this area in 1899."

"That would be the *Daily Gazette*," she said with authority, "but our stacks only go back two years."

"Is that the same newspaper building I passed back on First Street?" Victor inquired.

"Why, yes," the librarian smiled, seeming pleased that she was dealing with someone with a little knowledge. "That's the original—and only—newspaper here. And that's its original home, too."

"Do you know if they keep microfiche records?" asked Victor.

"That's interesting you should ask this," she explained, sounding like a teacher. "Someone else was here some months ago with the same request."

"You mean for a copy of the *Daily Gazette* from 1899?" Victor noticed his voice rising in anticipation of her reply. He hoped her response would be "no."

"Yes, 1899. What happened that year around here that's so important?" She smiled and suddenly took on a new, even softer, demeanor.

Now Victor didn't know what to say. "Oh, um, I'm just doing some research work." Then he remembered the microfiche. "Was this person able to find a copy of the paper that far back at the newspaper office?" Victor hoped she was satisfied with his answer.

"I'm not certain," she responded, apparently not suspicious, "but he never returned here, so perhaps he did find what he was looking for at the newspaper building."

Victor's anxiety rose again. *I'm probably too late,* he thought.

"Thanks very much. You've been very helpful." Victor smiled and stepped back toward the front door.

"Oh, you're welcome. Good luck." Her eyes sparkled, and she seemed like she meant it. *I'll need it*, Victor thought. He returned her smile and exited the library.

Victor walked quickly back up Park Street, toward the courthouse building, to First Avenue, and turned right. One short block more and he reached First Street. There on the corner was the newspaper building.

Victor wondered if the large brass doorknob he was turning was actually over a hundred years old, as he noticed the words *Published continuously since 1880* again. *I know they didn't have microfiche back then*, he thought as he opened the tall, heavy glass front door to the *Daily Gazette* building.

As Victor entered, his hopefulness rose. *This office surely didn't look like this a hundred years ago.* There were computer terminals everywhere. The *Daily Gazette* may have begun as a backwoods country paper, but it wasn't one anymore. *Maybe the 1899 edition is now little bits of magnetic data in one of these computers.*

A stand-up counter separated the entry area Victor stood in from the working area, which was the entire first floor of the building. Desks, chairs, papers, and people filled it all. Victor wondered where the printing presses were. The noise level belied the quiet, country-like look of the front of the building outside. Hustle and bustle were appropriate words to describe this scene inside.

A slim man in his fifties, shirt sleeves rolled up and wearing an old-fashioned green visor, walked from his desk across the room to the counter where Victor waited.

"What can I do for you?" he asked pleasantly.

"I'm looking for the August 4, 1899, edition of your paper," Victor said, more like a question than a statement.

"Um," the man squeezed his chin. "That'll take some doing."

Victor's hopes dropped as he waited for the man to think.

"You'll have to talk to Sara Jessup, the owner's wife. She was working on that."

Victor hoped "was working on" didn't mean that it never happened.

"Let's see…," the man turned and looked back over his shoulder. "Oh, there she is now, just sitting down at that desk by the window." The man pointed out a little woman who must have been in her seventies. He pulled open a low swinging door at a break in the countertop. Victor passed through, thanked the man, and walked a crooked path between desks and stacks of papers and boxes over to the older woman. He waited briefly at the side of her desk until she noticed him standing there.

"Oh, hello, young man. I'm sorry, my mind was on something else." She was a sweet woman who didn't act her age. She wore a flannel shirt and khaki slacks, but still looked feminine in them. She moved quickly and gave the impression that she could really take care of business around here. Victor felt he had met the right person to help him.

"That's all right," Victor smiled. "I just dropped in because I'm looking for a copy of your newspaper—the August 4, 1899, edition."

"Well, *that's* before my time," she giggled. "Can't say that about much these days, though."

"Oh, come on," Victor mused, "I'll bet you run circles around everyone here."

"Not like I used to," Sara smiled, seemingly looking for something. "A few years ago we had a big rush on here to conserve space. We had a warehouse full of every back issue and then we bought that microfilm machine so we could clear out all those papers. They were a fire hazard, too." Victor guessed that that's where the printing presses were now, in the warehouse.

"Let me see here; I had a logbook somewhere that lists all those old records." Victor's hopes jumped. "Nope; it's not here. Let me go check with Karl. Excuse me, young man, what's your name?"

"I'm sorry—it's Victor. Victor Truman."

"Excuse me, Victor. My name's Sara and I'll be right back. Just make yourself at home."

"Thank you."

Sara hopped up out of her chair and headed for a stairway that rose along the opposite wall to the second floor. He noticed how nimbly she climbed the stairs. *Good country stock*, he chuckled to himself, hoping he'd be that active and agile at her age.

Victor sat and wondered who was doing what among the dozen or so people surrounding him in this room. Looking down at Sara's desk, he surmised that she probably got more done than the others, even though she had no computer terminal, just an old rotary-type telephone. Her sharp, bouncy nature eliminated the need for high technology.

He heard her coming down the wooden stairway and smiled as she returned to her chair.

"My husband, Karl, can help you. He has the logbook in his office," she announced.

"That's great! Thank you, Mrs. Jessup, for your help." Victor stood as someone walked over to see her; Sara looked up at him and smiled as she gave him a little wave.

Victor held his hand up to signal good-bye and retraced her path over to the stairway. Climbing the stairs, he wondered if they were a century old, too. The top of the stairway opened into another large room upstairs. But this one was cut in two by a wall with a double-wide doorway through the center. He could see through to what appeared to be drafting tables with tall stools and long, well-lit glass tables where people were arranging and pasting pieces of paper.

The hall of the room he now stood in was actually one large office. There was a leather couch and coffee table to his left, against the wall; a wooden conference table with eight chairs around it in the center; stacks and stacks of boxes everywhere; and a grand, formidable desk facing him from the opposite side of the room. Except for the computer screen on the edge of the desk, and the art tables and lamps in the next room, this could be a working office of a hundred years ago.

A heavy, red-faced, jovial-looking man sitting behind the large desk stood and smiled. "How do you do. I'm Karl Jessup."

Victor walked quickly toward him. The two shook hands.

"How do you do, sir. I'm Victor Truman."

The man smiled and motioned with his hand. "Please, grab a chair."

Victor sat in one of the two wooden chairs trimmed in well-worn leather and said, "Mrs. Jessup's been very cordial, and I appreciate your time to help me."

Karl Jessup picked up a black notebook binder on his desk and smiled. "Sara said you're looking for a paper of ours from the late nineteenth century?"

It took a moment to register and then Victor replied, "Yes, sir. August 4, 1899."

"Eighteen hundred and ninety-nine. You sure weren't around then, young fella. Come to think of it, neither was I!" The old man chuckled and paged through the black notebook.

"No sir," Victor answered, feeling as if he owed the kindly old man an explanation. "I found an old..." *No, better not get into this*, Victor thought, "...I'm kind of a history buff and I want to see what it was like living here on my birthday at the turn of the century." Victor hoped he sounded convincing.

"Well, from what my daddy used to tell me, in many ways it was a whole lot better then than now." The old man was still leafing through the notebook. *Good*, Victor thought, *he bought it*.

"Here we go, young fella, you're in luck. We couldn't go all the way back to 1880 when my daddy started this paper. Seems he must not've saved the first ten years' worth or so. Prob'ly spent all his time just tryin' to keep his head above water."

"Oh, this is terrific," Victor smiled, sitting forward on the edge of the chair.

"It says here that the piece of film you want is in box number sixteen. Follow me." Mr. Jessup rose from his wooden swivel chair; it gave a loud creak.

Victor stood and followed Mr. Jessup across his office and through the doorway to what Victor had decided was the paste-up room. They walked past two rows of tilted art tables where six or seven people hurriedly worked. *It's a miracle how newspapers get put together so quickly, printed, and then dropped on doorsteps for miles around*, Victor thought. As they walked toward a closed door at the back of the building, Victor wondered how C. W. figured someone would even find a newspaper from 1899. What if Mr. Jessup's dad never did start saving them? *Victor,* he thought to himself, *you're really on a wild goose chase this time.*

Mr. Jessup opened the door and fumbled for a string overhead that turned on one bare lightbulb hanging from the center of the ceiling. They were in a large closet filled nearly to the top with dusty boxes, old typewriters, and an assortment of other antique-looking odds and ends.

"Let's see here, number sixteen." Mr. Jessup made a clucking noise with his tongue as he looked around the stacks of boxes. "It'll say MF16 on it, meaning microfilm," Mr. Jessup explained, stooping down and twisting sideways to read what was printed on some of the boxes.

"It's very kind of you to go to all this trouble," Victor said, apologetically.

"Don't mention it, young fella. That's why we got this contraption. But I don't think it's been used but once or twice. The Historical Society used it a lot awhile back for some book they put out, and then there was this other fella like you used it once."

"When was that?" Victor's forehead tightened.

"Oh, maybe a year ago. Come to think of it, I think he was interested in the same period as you."

Victor didn't like hearing that.

"Yep, I bet it was, 'cause here's number sixteen out of place on top of this here stack. Should'a been down there at the bottom of that one." Mr. Jessup chuckled. "Prob'ly was me who didn't return it to its proper place!" He reached up to take the box off the top of a stack that was just a bit taller than Mr. Jessup.

"Need a hand?" Victor moved over toward Mr. Jessup.

"Might not be a bad idea," Mr. Jessup explained. "Doc says I shouldn't be overdoin' it much." Victor reached up and slid box number MF16 off the others with a smile.

"Now where to?" he asked.

"Right out here. Follow me, young fella."

"Did that other fellow find what he was looking for?" Victor was worried that the secret was spoiled, that he was too late, or that whoever came before him took the piece of microfiche he wanted.

"I s'pose so, young fella. Don't recollect much about him now."

Victor followed Mr. Jessup to the opposite side of this end of the building.

"Here. You can put that down right here." Mr. Jessup pointed to a long table. It was cluttered with papers and pages of newsprint that Mr. Jessup was now gathering up in a pile and sliding to one end of the table. At the opposite end of the table sat something large and bulky, covered with a big, gray cloth-vinyl hood. Mr. Jessup grabbed the cover by two corners and lifted it up and off of what looked like an oversized computer screen with a glass plate table beneath it. Dust now swarmed around the area. Victor could see sunlit streaks of it in front of the window.

"There she is," said Mr. Jessup. Victor smiled.

"Now what we do here is take the film we want...." Mr. Jessup lifted the lid off the cardboard box. Inside were index dividers labeled first by year, then by month, and then by day. He walked his fingers to "1899," then skipped to "August," then with a thumb and index finger, pinched off four clear-plastic sheets.

"This should be what you want, young fella."

Something in Victor rose through his entire body and he stood up straighter and smiled.

"Now we place this little critter, top up, on this piece of glass here." Mr. Jessup laid the plastic sheet on the glass beneath the large screen and flipped a switch on the side of the machine. A bright light came on and the screen glowed.

"There! Now we just focus her." Mr. Jessup twisted a large black knob next to the glass plate and the image of an old newspaper page suddenly appeared in the screen. Victor's heart quickened.

"There you go, young fella. Just grab those two handles and slide it around to wherever you want." Mr. Jessup pulled a straight chair over in front of the machine for Victor to sit.

"Thank you very much," Victor said, his voice rising.

A complete daily paper was contained on one piece of plastic, about eight inches square. Victor slid the sheet around randomly at first. It was exciting to look back into time through this little plastic window.

There were several headlines that day, all in peculiarly small type: Appeal Against Clayton Now Comes to Naught, Says Rough Riders Will Fight Filipinos. Bishop Newman Dying. Christian Endeavor Convention Opened. Cyclone in this State.

Pages two and three displayed less urgent news and more local events: New American Rose Society Forms. Four Vessels Run Aground. A Temperance Tent Is Thronged. School Crew Wins. Robert G. Ervin Chosen. A Record-Breaking Trip.

And then...*there it was*:

Philanthropist Clement Watt
Dedicates New Town Orphanage

Philanthropist Clement Watt was greeted by a large audience of ladies and gentlemen on the grounds of the new orphanage on Third Street between Third and Fourth Avenues yesterday afternoon, when he delivered the dedication oration.

The new 6,500 square foot Children's Home was profusely decorated with the national colors, the state and city seals, and "Old Glory."

The exercises were on lines that have characterized previous similar occasions, and the orator, whose theme was familial ties and aspirations of high degrees, held the close attention of his audience, and judging by their generous applause, he evidently obtained their sympathy on this subject.

The unassuming orator was escorted to the platform by Mayor Quincy, accompanied by the Rev. Dr. Lindsey of St. Paul's Church, as chaplain of the day; Master Vincent Collins, the reader of the Declaration of Independence; Gov. Underwood; Mr. John Wheeler, the new Children's Home Administrator; and the Hon. Patrick A. Galvin.

The Municipal band opened the exercises with an overture introducing several national airs, following which divine blessing was invoked by Chaplain Lindsey, who returned thanks that "We are bound together as one people in love and patriotism with the cords of kindness and fraternal affection."

Master Collins read the Declaration of Independence with perfect enunciation, and so distinctly that every syllable was heard across all parts of the grounds. He was heavily applauded, and at the conclusion of the exercises was warmly congratulated by the gentlemen on the platform.

Mr. Thomas E. Clifford sang Keller's "American Hymn," and then Mayor Quincy introduced Mr. Clement Watt as the orator of the day.

Mr. Watt was cordially received. Stepping forward to the

bunting-covered porch rail, he cleared his throat, paused, and calmly gazed about the audience, some seated and others standing on the spacious lawn surrounding the porch. He spoke as follows:

"How fortunate that it is I who can provide this humble home, albeit a substitute one, for those children who find themselves lacking what so many others take for granted: a home—father, mother, brothers, and sisters. May this feeble substitute provide at least for their basic needs of food, shelter, and companionship until which time they venture forth from this place, out amongst the world, on their own.

"When such time comes, it is my ardent wish that each of these children comes to question what he, or she, sees in this world, in people's faces, and, not the least, in his or her own mind.

"It was my greatest fortune to have been directed and guided in mid-life to this grander form of thought of which I speak here to you today. May the young children who come to call this place home seek what appears on the surface to be the impossible, for then they surely shall meet a teacher such as favored me.

"For things are not what they seem. In the world's broad field of battle, in the bivouac of Life, be not like dumb, driven cattle! Be a hero in the strife! Trust no future, howe'er pleasant, let the dead past bury its dead! Act, act in the living present. Heart within, and God o'er head."

Then he proclaimed, "I leave this well to show the way to those who seek direction out of the world's broad field of battle."

With those brief words, Mr. Watt slowly and deliberately descended the decorated stairs of the porch, and across the lawn in front of the Municipal band, to a white-canvas covered object approximately four feet in width and six feet in height. With a smile, he slowly pulled away the canvas to reveal a bronze statue of a covered water well. Its roof bears an inscription of Mr. Watt's closing words.

With this, the exuberant audience applauded, cheered, and several whistled. The band then concluded the exercises with "My Country 'Tis of Thee."

The large new Children's Home provides perpetual care for up to thirty-five orphans until they reach the age of majority. The Home's operation is entirely funded by a perpetual trust established and endowed by millionaire-industrialist Mr. Watt who designated the local First National Bank to act as Trustee.

Mr. Watt's biography is a mystery to most. He has always politely declined personal interviews. Local accounts suggest that he makes his home on the East Coast, is a friend and confidant to kings and presidents, and that he founded and heads several major business enterprises and conglomerates. It is rumored that he anonymously establishes and perpetually endows orphanages across the nation, such as the one dedicated here yesterday. Apparently in his late forties, and said to be a widower, Mr. Watt travels extensively but returns here more or less regularly on a monthly basis. He keeps a private room at Emma's boarding house on Park Street.

"Then it *is* true," Victor whispered, breathing deeply. The headstone wasn't a hoax. Clement Watt did leave a posthumous clue to a secret message. Victor was on the trail now. He could feel his pulse beating.

But what if Mr. Jessup didn't have this microfiche machine? What if the August 4, 1899, issue of the *Daily Gazette* had never been saved?

Victor was staring out the window, wondering about all this, when he suddenly realized there were only two people here in the upper floor room now: a teenage boy emptying waste paper cans, and himself. He looked across the room at a clock on the wall. Six-forty.

"I missed the van!" Victor said aloud.

The boy looked over at him and said, "Beg your pardon?"

"Oh, I lost track of the time," Victor explained, half to himself. He got up from his chair, walked across the room to the doorway, and looked into Mr. Jessup's office.

Mr. Jessup was writing, and stopped mid-sentence to look up at Victor. "That must've been some issue, son! I guess you found what you were lookin' for."

"Yes sir," Victor said apologetically. "I'm very sorry to keep you waiting; I just lost track of the time."

"Oh, you didn't hold me up none, young fella, I'd'a booted you out if you were."

"Thank you. You've been very kind. I'd like to copy down a short article from that paper. I could come back tomorrow."

"Oh poppycock! We got a machine that'll do that, too." The old man strained his neck toward the doorway and called into the adjoining room: "Billy? You in there?"

"Yes, Mr. Jessup, coming." The young boy came into the office with Victor and Mr. Jessup. "Yessir?"

"Billy, do you know how to run a copy from those microfilms?"

"Yes, Mr. Jessup."

"Good. This fella here's going to show you what he wants a copy of."

"Thank you. That's terrific," Victor said.

He and Billy went over to the projector and Victor pointed out the article.

"It'll just take me a few minutes," said Billy shyly.

Victor sensed that Billy would rather be left alone and walked back into Mr. Jessup's half of the upstairs floor. Mr. Jessup was writing again but stopped and gave Victor his attention with a smile.

"You've been so very kind," Victor told him. "People aren't as kind and thoughtful where I come from as you folks are around here."

"Oh, you from New York?" The old man chuckled.

"No, I'm from around Los Angeles—just outside—the San Fernando Valley," Victor explained.

"I thought you were from here. You mean I ain't going to get a newspaper subscription outta ya?" The old man laughed at his own joke.

"Well, I kind of *do* wish I lived here, but we're on vacation."

The old man tilted his head questioningly.

"Oh," Victor explained, "my wife and I are staying at the Grand Hotel on a vacation for a few days."

"Pretty fancy, young fella, the Grand Hotel!"

"Oh, yes," Victor explained again, "we won this trip in a sales contest." Victor couldn't bring himself to admit that his wife did all the work and won the trip.

"What'd'ya sell?" the old man asked.

"Real estate."

"Guess you folks have some mighty high prices out there."

"Yes sir, we certainly do."

There was a pause, and Victor took this opportunity to continue his search for clues.

"Mr. Jessup? Do you know of a Mr. Clement Watt from around here?"

"Clement Watt." The old man leaned back in his chair, looked toward the ceiling, and smiled.

"I haven't heard that name in many, many years." He gazed across the room and Victor's hopes rose again.

"Yes, Clement Watt...."

Victor could tell the old man's thoughts were building and that he was about to gain some good information. He wished he had asked sooner.

The old man seemed to have collected his thoughts, sorted them out, and was ready to present them to Victor in a concise, coherent package. With a twinkle in his eye, he looked at Victor, sat forward, and clasped his hands in front of him on the desk.

CHAPTER 5

"Clement Watt was a legend," Mr. Jessup began, "and a delightful mystery all rolled up into one. He was loved by all, but no one seemed to know him very well. He wasn't secretive by any means, but he seemed to be everywhere and nowhere at the same time." The old man squinted his eyes and raised his forehead as if to demonstrate an enigma. Victor could tell that he was enjoying his reminiscence.

"How do you mean?" Victor asked, moving forward on the edge of his chair.

"Clement Watt was a rich man. A very, *very* wealthy man. And none of us, I suspect, knew the half of it. We'd hear a little bit here that he traded in the commodity markets, and another little bit there that he owned big businesses, and none of the bits were ever the same. It seemed there was just no end to Clement Watt's doin's. But you never would have guessed it if you didn't know him, and if you did know him, he'd never talk about his accomplishments."

"Did *you* know him?" Victor's eyes widened.

Just then, Billy came through the door, but didn't interrupt.

The old man looked over Victor's head. "You got that copy for my friend here, Billy?"

"Yes, sir. It came out nice." Billy was proud of his work.

Victor turned in his chair and Billy held out the copy. Victor took it, and looked at the article as if it were a picture of Christine. Christine! Victor remembered that he missed the van and didn't know how he would get back to the Grand Hotel. Before he figured it all out, however, he'd better call her. But not yet. He had tapped a vein here with Karl Jessup that was leading to what seemed to be a gold mine.

"Thanks very much. This is a perfect copy," Victor said.

"You're welcome." Billy felt a little more important and appreciated the attention.

Victor turned back toward the old man and continued: "So you knew Clement Watt personally?"

The old man laughed. "Well, I knew him as good as a twelve-year-old boy could know a man in his seventies. I met him with my daddy on several occasions, and I saw him around town here many times growing up. My daddy always spoke fondly of Mr. Watt and would tell me things about him. Thinkin' back now, I believe I knew more about that man from the few times I was actually near him. This sounds mighty peculiar, but he had a presence about him that you could just feel. He could calm you down just bein' near him."

"You mean he'd try to calm people down? How?" Victor looked confused.

"No, it was just his way, his manner. He spoke soft, but he spoke with authority. You knew he knew what he was talkin' about, that's it. No gossipin', no chitchat. He always had a purpose to what he said."

"Then you had conversations with him?" Victor asked.

"Well, no, but one time I was next after him at the barber shop. That's the time I heard him speak the most. The barber was used to gossip talk and politics talk and such, and I remember old Mr. Watt just sat there and had a pleasant smile on his lips. I could tell he didn't want to talk gossip or politics, but it didn't bother him that the others were. He just sat there quiet and happy, enjoying and taking it all in."

"But you said he was extremely wealthy?" Victor was digging.

"Oh, he was. My daddy used to mention the big corporation he started, and the boards he sat on. It took me awhile to figure out what sitting on a board meant," he chuckled. "He wasn't here all that much, and my daddy told me he was off to Chicago or New York or Boston and such. But you never would've known it."

"Well, didn't he like to talk big business or talk about money?"

"Not that I heard that Saturday morning in the barber shop. He wasn't a flaunty type and didn't even own a house here. Whenever he was in town here, he stayed at Emma's boarding house down on Park Street. He had a permanent room there, my daddy said.

"I saw him there once, too. I was walkin' down the street and he was tendin' to some flowers in the front yard. Down on his hands and knees. He looked up and said, 'Hello, young man. Isn't it a beautiful day?' Bein' a kid, I was surprised a grown-up talked to me like a grown-up, and it took me a minute to answer back.

"'Yes sir,' I said, and just stood there. I remember thinkin' he must've thought I was dumb or somethin'. I really liked him for treatin' me like an adult and didn't want him to think he wasted his time on me."

"Karl? You up there?" Sara's voice echoed up the stairway.

Not now! Victor hoped his face didn't show what he was thinking.

"I gotta go put supper on," she announced from downstairs.

Good! Victor thought, *maybe she'll go home to cook and leave Karl alone.*

"I'll be down presently, Sara," he called back.

Darn! Victor knew his time was short. Here he was getting first-hand information. Maybe he could get another clue from Mr. Jessup.

"It mentions Emma's boarding house in the paper," Victor held up the copy Billy had made. "Did Emma know Mr. Watt very well?"

"Oh, I 'spect so, but she's been long gone now. I do believe her daughter runs the place now, though. It's still there where I saw him that day, up and over on Park Street."

Victor knew his time was about to end, and he felt his discovery was safe with Mr. Jessup (after all, anyone in the world was free to see it!), so he asked his Big Question:

"Mr. Jessup, I happened on an old cemetery out by the Grand Hotel that isn't used much anymore."

"Oh, yeah, the old Civil War Cemetery. My momma and daddy's buried there. Haven't been out there for many years, though."

"Well, apparently Mr. Watt is buried there." Victor waited for a reaction or comment.

"He is? You know, now that you mention it, it seems I do recollect hearing that fact some time back." The old man rubbed the back of his neck.

"Yes, and there's a message on his headstone. It says 'Take the first step....'" Victor waited.

The old man looked at Victor, waiting for him to finish. When Victor just looked back expectantly, Mr. Jessup said, "That's it? Nothin' else?"

"No, nothing else, just 'Take the first step.'"

The old man chuckled. "That sounds like old Mr. Watt. Very few words, but words with meanin'. That's what I was tellin' you. He was like that. Say, let me see that copy you got there."

Victor handed him the article. He smiled as he quickly read it. "My daddy wrote this." He continued reading, and smiling.

"That was before my time, but that orphanage's been a landmark around here. It's on Watt Street, you know. They named it after him soon after the orphanage went in, my daddy told me."

"Karl! Do you want supper tonight or not?" Mrs. Jessup's voice coming up the stairway was playful, but she meant business.

"Yes, dear heart. I'm comin'," Mr. Jessup called back as he stood and handed the copy back to Victor with a fond smile on his face.

"Thank you very much, Mr. Jessup. You've been more than kind to me."

"Oh, nonsense, young fella. You brought up some good memories for me."

The two left the office and walked down the stairway to a waiting Sara near the front door.

"Thank you, Mrs. Jessup, for sharing your husband. He's helped me very much this afternoon—er, evening," Victor said, looking out through the glass door.

"Glad we could help," she smiled. "Now I've got to get this young'un home and feed him or he turns grumpy and cantankerous on me."

The old man grumbled under his breath and Victor chuckled.

"Oh, young fella, I was just thinkin'. I just remembered somethin' old Mr. Watt said to me that day out in Emma's front yard. He told me to never believe that somethin' couldn't be done. 'Don't believe it if somebody else tells you that, and don't believe it even if your own mind tells you that,' he said. I had an inklin' that he had told me somethin' very important—especially to a young'un. I remembered that for a long time. And you know, it got me through some tough times. Helped save this paper one rough spell we went through here. Remember that, Sara?"

"Yes, dear. Now if you don't move along, it'll be bedtime."

"You goin' back to the Grand Hotel?" Mr. Jessup asked Victor.

"Well, I don't have a car, and the last van back left...." Victor realized he had been irresponsible the way he had lost track of time and missed the van. This could be serious; he could be stranded here. He felt warm and embarrassed.

"Oh, go over to the hotel. It's real nice. Just go up one block to Park, then over one block more to Second Avenue. Tell ole Walton I said 'Hey.'"

"Thanks again, folks. You've been terrific." Victor smiled and held up his hand to say good-bye.

Sara and Karl waved back, locked arms, turned, and walked the opposite direction down First Street. They looked very sweet together. Victor hoped he and Christine would grow old together like that.

It was still fairly light out, but evening wasn't far off. He had to call Christine, but right now, even more importantly, he had to find a home for the night. Victor felt that something big was about to happen to him here, that his life was about to take on a major new direction.

He walked up First Avenue toward the courthouse. There were few cars on the road, and even fewer pedestrians. Everyone seemed to already be home for dinner.

Victor was lonesome for Christine. He reminded himself again that he'd better call her soon or she'd be worried.

As he arrived at Park Street, he looked up, across the street, atop the courthouse where lights illuminated its grand white tower. What a picture. Victor took it all in: A balmy summer's evening in a small American town. Brick and pastel-colored buildings lined up, quaint and cozy, along the short streets. Two young boys riding their bicycles down the front steps of the towering courthouse across the street (something they would never do during business hours), and the bright-white tower silhouetted against the dark-blue sky of dusk.

Up and down Park Street, on both sides of the courthouse, hundreds of huge old trees with their dark, broad, irregular forms slowly disappeared into the looming night. *This is the kind of small-town-America scene Norman Rockwell captured so perfectly*, Victor thought.

He crossed First Avenue and walked by the shops and offices along Park Street until he reached Second Avenue. Just across Second stood the Park Hotel. What a grand building; it was a large, two-story, gray-brick structure with six high, slender, arched windows across the front of each floor. Eight tall square white posts lining the edge of the sidewalk supported a large white wooden balcony that sheltered pedestrians below. White picket railing decorated the front edge of the balcony and created a sitting deck for rooms on the second floor. Brass gas lamps hung on both sides of each window lintel, so at night the Park Hotel became a shining beacon.

Victor could almost hear a honky-tonk piano's tinny tones playing "Camptown Races."

He opened one of the two eight-foot framed-glass entry doors and could feel the weight of the dark-green velvet curtains that hung on the inside. Another time machine: Victor stepped into the late 1800s.

A large gas chandelier spilled down out of the vaulted ceiling over what looked more like an opulent private great room than a hotel lobby. Dozens of tiny gas flames glowing from the ends of its ornately shaped brass tubing filled the room with a nice, quiet, flickering glow.

Heavy, rich, sedately colored fabrics were everywhere: in the chairs, couches, love seat, curtains, and rugs. It was a grand room. Dark wood paneling and old oil landscapes decorated its long walls.

"Good evening, sir." Victor turned to the back corner of the lobby, to a man standing behind a polished dark-wood registration desk. Victor wasn't certain the man was speaking to him at first. All the thick, soft furnishings in this room soaked up sounds, so his salutation reached Victor almost as a whisper. When he realized the man was speaking to him, Victor smiled and walked across the large room.

He was a thin, average-looking man in a dark brown business suit with a stiff white shirt and boring tie. He stood erect and proper behind the registration desk as if it were a symphony conductor's podium, arms and hands outstretched, clasping the smooth wooden railing that framed the top of the counter. A small brass lamp with a green glass shade illuminated the large leather registration book. The countertop was dark green marble with small golden veins coursing through it.

"Hello, my name's Victor Truman and I need a room this evening, please." *I wonder if he'll let me check in without a coat and tie,* Victor wondered.

"Very good, sir," responded the man on cue. Victor was relieved. "A room for one?"

"Yes, just me. I missed the last shuttle back to the Grand Hotel, so I thought I'd spend the night in town," Victor explained.

"Welcome to the Park Hotel," he said, not noticing, or possibly ignoring, Victor's attempt at conversation. "Do you have any luggage that you'll need carried up to your room?" the man mechanically continued.

From what he just told the man, Victor thought the answer was obvious, but he responded anyway: "No, no luggage."

"If you'll kindly complete our register," the man requested, holding out a pen. The pages were already facing forward. Victor took the pen and looked to the most recently completed line of information for guidance. A new page had just begun. The top line contained the handwriting of a Mr. or Mrs. Keith Andersen of Grants Pass, Oregon, who registered just this morning. Victor guessed Mrs. Andersen wrote this: the handwriting was light and flowing, as if a feminine hand had made it. "11:30 A.M." was written by another hand. Probably Walton's.

Victor wrote in the information and considered how much nicer this was than saying all these personal facts out loud to a hotel clerk who keyed them into a computer. Much more civilized this way. Then Victor wondered if he could use a credit card.

"Can I put this on my Visa card?" Victor held it out.

"Of course, sir." The man took the card and went to work behind a big square wooden box that covered the counter just to his right.

Victor realized he didn't know how much a room here would cost, but he didn't have much choice. And after all, Mr. Jessup recommended the Park Hotel, and he didn't seem to be the least bit extravagant.

Then Victor remembered: "Are you Walton?"

"Yes, sir, I am," Walton answered, looking up with a puzzled expression.

"Well, hello, Walton. Mr. Karl Jessup over at the *Daily Gazette* told me to tell you 'Hey!'" The word 'hey' didn't sound right in the lobby of the Park Hotel; much too crude.

Walton looked slightly embarrassed, perhaps even a little perturbed, but managed to respond: "Tell Mr. Jessup thank you."

Victor guessed the down-home demeanor of Karl Jessup ruffled Walton's image of his impeccable self. He bet he had just been used by Mr. Jessup to once again play a game Mr. Jessup was fond of: teasing ole Walton. Victor smiled.

Walton produced a credit card receipt for Victor to sign, and then said perfunctorily, "Your room is sixty-five dollars a night, Mr. Truman, and I shall total this statement upon your departure. Your room is number 205, upstairs."

That sounded reasonable. Walton handed Victor a heavy key with a very large square head. "205" was stamped in it.

"Thank you, Walton. And where can I get some dinner now?"

"You may dine until nine o'clock in our dining room." Walton extended his hand toward a wide curtained archway leading from the lobby. Next to it stood what must have been a nine-foot tall grandfather's clock. The big black hands showed eight o'clock. Something in the big clock clicked, and out came the first of eight mighty gongs. They weren't loud, just strong and deep. Walton was writing in the register. *Probably filling in the time I checked in*, Victor surmised.

"Is there a telephone nearby?" Victor asked.

"There's one in your room," Walton replied, looking up, "and also a public telephone in the hallway between the dining room and the lounges."

"Thanks." Victor disappeared through the archway.

He was now in a narrow area, a kind of anteroom, between the hotel lobby and the dining room. A dark-wood rostrum stood unattended next to a matching curtained archway opposite the one he had just come through. Victor could see into the dining room. It was old and elegant, too. A stairway as wide as the room led up a flight to the hotel's rooms.

A middle-aged woman, her hair in a tight bun, wearing a full black skirt and starched white blouse came through the archway from the dining room. A wonderful aroma followed her in: good home cooking.

"May I seat you for dinner?" She had a soothing, motherly quality to her voice.

"Yes, please. I'm dining alone," Victor said.

"Very well. Please, follow me."

The aroma was even better in the dining room. Fresh, hot bread wasn't far away.

The dining room was as large as the lobby, but the light was dimmer in here. Curtains were drawn in the windows. A glass lamp with two burning candles sat in the middle of each of forty or more round tables in the room. Cane chairs with leather seats circled each table. There were perhaps twenty diners, all carrying on conversations, yet the room was pleas-antly quiet and subdued. The woman led Victor to a smaller round table with two chairs next to the front window. It was away from other diners and Victor appreciated that.

"This looks perfect," Victor said, "Thanks very much."

"Your waiter will serve you presently. Enjoy your meal."

Victor sat and parted the window curtains slightly with his fingers. The gas lamps on the front of the hotel lit up the sidewalk outside. A couple strolled by. The line of handsome gas street lamps along Park Street stood at attention as far down the sidewalk as Victor could see.

And what a menu! Victor's eyebrows rose as he saw his choices for dinner: Buttermilk fried chicken with butter beans and glazed sweet potatoes. River bottom gumbo with butter-milk cornbread. Country smoked ham with red-eye gravy, boiled new potatoes covered in lemon garlic butter, and snap beans cooked with hambone.

He made his selection quickly (the gumbo), placed his order with the waiter, and then left the dining room by anoth-er archway in the back wall for the telephone. Halfway down this hallway to the lounges there were low alcoves in the wall, each with a seat, wooden shelf, and telephone. Victor sat in the first one and pulled his Grand Hotel key and most of his change from his pocket. *Good, the phone number's on it.* He fed a dime into the slot and punched in the number. "Grand Hotel, good evening," the voice said. Victor couldn't believe he had gotten through for just a dime.

"Room 123 please."

"Hello."

"Hi, sweetie, it's me."

"Victor! Where are you? I've been very worried."

"I knew you would be, and I'm sorry."

"Where are you?"

"I just checked into the Park Hotel over here in town. I'm in room 205."

"Why? What happened?"

"I'm really onto something here, Chrissy. Remember C. W.? Well, he really existed, and I think he did leave a message hidden somewhere around here."

"What did you find?"

"The date that was hidden in the decoration on the headstone was the same date of the local paper that carried an article about C. W.—his name's Clement Watt. He was a very wealthy man around here. They even named a street after him. But he wasn't a celebrity or anything like that, he was actually kind of a quiet, private person, but very powerful—in a good way."

"You sure this isn't just a coincidence?"

Coincidence? Coincidence! He had forgotten to ask Mr. Jessup about the yacht named *Coincidental*. The van driver said it belonged to the orphanage. "No way, I *know* this isn't just a coincidence!"

"Well, when will you be home?"

"Tomorrow. I have another clue to check out and I'll start first thing tomorrow morning. I'll catch a hotel van on one of its trips into town here."

"I'm so glad you're all right, Victor."

"I love you, honey."

"I love you, too, Victor; and if anything ever happened to you—"

"Well, something has, or is about to, and it's great!"

"I hope so. Good night, Victor. I love you."

Victor's new surge of enthusiasm overtook his appetite, but he remembered the gumbo as he returned to the dining room. He re-read the *Daily Gazette* newspaper article between bites. The old clock in the hotel lobby was bonging out nine o'clock as he headed up the stairway to room 205.

When Victor opened the door he immediately thought of his grandmother's house. There's a certain smell that homes in humid climates take on. This room had it, too. Victor liked it and took in an extra deep breath.

The room was small but full. It contained a double bed with an old-fashioned quilt, two bedside tables with ornate antique lamps on white lace doilies, a small clock radio on one, a telephone on the other. A three-drawer dresser and mirror stood next to the room's only window, across from the bed. A proud old three-rung chair stood next to the small wall closet next to the bathroom door.

No television, Victor noticed. No luggage, no clothes, and no toothbrush, either. This was new for Victor—not being prepared. But what could he do now? All of this just sort of happened. And he was glad it did.

Nine o'clock at night. No TV, nothing to read, nowhere to go. The radio. Let's see what's on the radio around here at night. He turned the tuner knob all the way to the left. Slowly turning the knob to the right, the needle moved more than an inch before the first station came in clearly. Elevator music. *Keep going.* An inch more, hard-core country music. *Turn it some more.* Forties big band era music. *That sounded nice. Let's try another.* News. *No.* Two inches more, close to the right edge of the dial, a call-in talk station. *Let's see what this is like.*

"Welcome back to 'The Garden Variety Show.'" *Oh, brother, a garden talk show. And the rest of the country thinks Californians are crazy.*

"Our special guest tonight is the chief rosarian of the famed Huntington Gardens in San Marino."

San Marino? That's right near where I live!

"Our topic this evening—roses—has lit up the station switchboard, but keep trying to get through. The number to call is 213-555-BUDS. That's 555-2837."

Five, five, five, B-U-D-S? Oh, come on. Wait a minute! Two, one, three area code? That's Los Angeles! I must have heard that wrong.

"Hello? You're on the line with Gary Morgan and our special guest rosarian tonight on KPLA."

KPLA! Then that is Los Angeles! Wait a minute, am I in some time warp, or going nuts, or what?

"Yes, I'd like to ask your guest about the American Rose Society?"

What? I don't believe this! I remember seeing an article about the American Rose Society in that newspaper. Victor pulled the copy from his pocket, even though he knew the rose article he remembered seeing had not been copied. *This is just too coincidental!* Victor thought of the yacht again. He felt goose bumps slowly spread over his back, shoulders, and arms.

"The American Rose Society was founded in 1899 to encourage research and help dispense information on all aspects of roses. The society began in Louisiana and is a thriving organization today with many local volunteer consultants you may contact for help and advice."

Here I am all the way across the country listening to a radio station back home. This must be that phenomenon where the radio signal skips over vast distances. But it's so clear! I've heard of this, but never had it happen to me before.

"Thank you. And let's go to our next caller, please."

"Hello?"

"Yes, you're on the air. What is your question for our guest?"

"Is it true there's no such thing as a blue rose?"

"That's correct, there are no blue roses. Not many people are aware of this fact. The so-called modern era of rose growing began in 1867 when the first hybrid tea rose—the class that dominates present-day rose gardens—was introduced. Exciting new hybrids of new colors and bicolors began to flourish at the turn of the century. But a sky-blue, true-blue, or delphinium-blue rose has never been grown. Some hybrids such as the Blue Girl, in 1964, and the Blue Nie of 1981 are actually lavender-colored roses. There are also mauve, gray, and purple roses sometimes incorrectly called blue roses, but there is no true-blue rose. The Japanese and Australians are spending vast amounts of money conducting gene-splicing experiments, using genes from petunias and other plant families, but there still is no true-blue rose."

"I'm afraid we're out of time tonight. This is Gary Morgan thanking our special guest this evening from the Huntington Gardens in San Marino. Tune in next week to 'The Garden Variety Show,' same time, right here on KPLA, Los Angeles. Stay tuned for news, sports, and weather with Mary Ashley."

I still can't believe this! Victor left the radio on to see what other surprises lay in store. He fell asleep mentally repeating the words, "Take the first step," and trying to imagine how a true-blue rose would look.

CHAPTER 6

Victor awoke to birds chirping. Actually, one yapping blue jay in particular woke him. He got out of bed, walked to the window, and pushed the curtains aside. Beautiful. Absolutely breathtaking. What a morning! Humid skies definitely are more dramatic. There's more substance to them somehow: more clouds, more moisture, more feeling. Maybe the beautiful skies are why people can tolerate humidity.

The sun was red, rising behind white bands of clouds. A pink cast dribbled over the landscape. Thick, moist shafts of pink sunlight shot through the trees and into the glistening green grass beneath them in the park across the street.

This was a very special day. Victor felt it.

He phoned the front desk and Walton answered. *Doesn't he ever go home?*

"Good morning, Walton. This is Victor Truman in two-oh-five."

"Good morning, sir."

"Walton, is there a little gift shop in the hotel?"

"Of course, sir."

"Good. Would they have razors and such?"

"We have a full selection of toiletries, sir."

"Great. Could I get some items delivered to my room this morning?"

"What items would you like?"

"Let's see. A razor, toothbrush, toothpaste, and a comb." Yep, that should do it.

"And would you like to order breakfast in your room this morning, sir?"

"Is the dining room open for breakfast?"

"It opens in twenty minutes."

"Then I'll come down to eat. Thank you."

"Very good, sir. Your sundries shall be brought up presently."

"Thanks very much, Walton, you're a champ."

That caught Walton off guard. He cleared his throat. "Thank you, I'm sure."

"Bye." Victor hung up and smiled. Poor Walton.

Waiting for his supplies to arrive, he realized that the radio had been on all night. He turned the volume up, secretly hoping that KPLA would be on.

"And that was the legendary Eddy Arnold singing his classic, 'Make the World Go Away.' It's seven-forty-five here on Country Classic Radio, WCCR, all the classics, all the time, twenty-four hours, where it's going to be a hot one today. The weatherman says it should hit the mid- to high-eighties today with the humidity doin' the same. Better make an extra pitcher of iced tea or lemonade today; it's gonna be a scorcher. Now see if you can guess the title of this ole tune from the Queen of Country Music, Miss Loretta Lynn."

Twenty-four hours. That means KPLA's signal drowned out this strong local station last night. Coincidental? Victor thought of the yacht again.

His toiletries arrived and Victor showered, shaved, and "dressed" quickly. *Not too wrinkled*, he thought, looking into the mirror at his shirt. *Maybe I'll buy one of those big floppy short-sleeved tourist numbers I've seen so many of on this trip.* He packed his new supplies in the paper bag in which they arrived. Then he remembered Jeffrey and Nicole. *The kids always liked the little shampoo, conditioner, and body lotion bottle sets from hotels. Nikki will be especially pleased with this plastic shower cap. And Jeff likes postcards.* Victor pulled the top drawer in the nightstand open and there it was: a set of stationery and a color postcard of the Park Hotel.

After checking out and thanking Walton, Victor went into the dining room for breakfast. The curtains were pulled back and sunlight streamed in. The abundance of sunshine made this a completely different room than it had appeared last night. There were only six people having breakfast—three couples scattered about the big room. Victor requested the same table from the night before, at the front window.

What a view: the long sidewalk trailing off, a car here and there, an occasional pedestrian. To the left across the street was the grand brick courthouse, and everywhere else was park and what looked like miles of trees, grass, and leaves. Everything green, and every shade of it.

Waiting for his breakfast of scrambled eggs, biscuits and gravy, and sausage links, Victor re-read the article, something he had done twenty times since that copy was made not much over twelve hours ago.

Emma's boarding house and the orphanage: the only two leads he had. Finding Mr. Jessup and his microfiche machine was a blessing. Deep, muffled tones from the big clock made their way through the dining room. It was nine o'clock.

Victor laid the article up against the plate opposite his—which would be Christine's if she were here—and examined every word of it as he enjoyed his meal.

Victor paid his bill and asked the waitress if she knew where Emma's boarding house was located.

"Oh, yes, it's just two blocks farther down Park Street here. The hotel's on Second Avenue, then Third," she pointed out through the window, away from the courthouse, "then Fourth Avenue, and there's Emma's."

"Does Emma run it?" Victor asked, testing her knowledge.

"Oh, I don't think so anymore."

Victor thanked her and left the hotel. He felt like he was forgetting something, looked down at the little white paper bag in his hand, touched the article folded in his pocket, and smiled. Nope, he had everything he needed to find what he was looking for. Then he smiled again when he realized he didn't actually know what it was he was looking for. But he knew he was in the right place to find it.

It was just after nine o'clock, but the air was already warm and heavy. The white clouds were billowing now. Victor could still hear the blue jay that woke him as he passed the end of the hotel building and headed along the sidewalk to Emma's.

A row of shops and businesses lined Park Street from the hotel to Third Avenue. One was Parker's General Merchandise. Parker's was a wooden two-story building that seemed a bit out of place along this section of Park Street. It was less formal than all the other brick structures and looked friendlier somehow. It created its own atmosphere when one walked under its enormous deep wooden porch that began from the second story window and enveloped the entire sidewalk in front of the building, all the way out to the street. It was almost like being indoors under here. Victor could easily look through the large window panes and all around the store since there was no glare under this voluminous porch.

Victor peered in, first to see if Parker's was open, and then to determine if they had men's shirts.

Yes, Parker's was open: A woman with a shopping bag came out of the store. Now, do they have men's shirts? Yes; over a doorway through the back wall was a sign: Men's Women's Children's Clothing Upstairs.

Victor went in.

He came out carrying a larger bag than he entered with. He also was wearing a new shirt: a slightly oversized, square-tail, short-sleeve style with a subdued print that looked less touristy than the loud floral designs he had been seeing.

Feeling refreshed now, he continued down Park Street where he left off.

Crossing Third Avenue, everything changed: He was in an all-residential neighborhood now with one long row of antique homes. Every one of them had to have been built in the mid- to late-1800s; the telltale architecture was outstanding. The Queen Anne style abounded: wooden homes embellished with high porches; ornamental white railings, posts, and turrets; stone chimneys; steep-roofed dormers; scalloped wood siding; and an abundance of fine, detailed woodwork.

Old, stout magnolia and oak trees stood in the front yards of most of these homes, protecting the family that lived inside. Their strong roots had reached out and beyond the front yards over the years and now made large sections of the sidewalk twist, turn, and undulate as if a river flowed beneath it. A walk through time. Victor smiled and was coming to Fourth Avenue, and the end house.

It was the belle of the ball. *They saved the best for last,* Victor thought. This house was a palace. It stood taller than the mighty old trees that occupied its yard. Every other house on the block was diminished by this old grand dame.

Two flights of stairs ten feet wide led up to a deep, covered porch that encircled the entire house. The porch had an extra gazebo with its own spiral roof jutting out toward a huge magnolia tree at the front left corner. Above the porch and gazebo roofs towered the second story. Its rooms had their own covered balconies with white posts, railings, and gingerbread decoration. The third-story windows' decorative white wood frames were tucked under the front roof's many gables.

The separate roof of the home's rear section also rose three stories, had two brick chimneys of its own, and flaunted a white balcony railing running its entire length.

Best of all, there was a small rectangular wooden sign with green script lettering planted in the lawn next to the oversized porch: Emma's Boarding House.

Victor took a deep breath and climbed the eleven steps to the top of the porch. Then it was another good four paces to the front door itself. The big porch could have been a room of its own. It had wicker chairs, benches, coffee tables with glass tops, and a round table-and-chairs set. A broad wooden swing chair, big enough for three adults, hung from two thick chains in the circular gazebo-corner of the porch.

He pulled back the screen door and rapped lightly three times on the front door. Moving back a step, he closed the screen door and watched the leaded glass panes in the door. A few seconds later there was movement behind the glass.

"Hello." A handsome middle-aged woman in a simple, trim house dress and white apron answered the door.

"Hi. My name's Victor Truman and I'm doing a little historical research. Mr. Karl Jessup who owns the *Daily Gazette* newspaper was very helpful yesterday, and an article I found from 1899 led me here to Emma's boarding house."

"Oh, my. Eighteen ninety-nine, that's way before my time."

"Are you the proprietor, ma'am, may I ask?" Victor wasn't quite sure how to go about this. He didn't want to sound pushy.

"Yes, I'm Emma's granddaughter."

"How do you do?" Victor nodded his head. "In this article I found," Victor took it from his pocket, unfolded it, and held it out, "it tells of a man named Clement Watt when he dedicated the orphanage here in town. It also says that when in town he lived at Emma's boarding house. Would this be that same house where he stayed?" *Seems too good to be true, but please say yes.*

"Yes, this is the house. Would you wait a moment, please?"

"Yes I will. Thank you." *This is the house! Thank you, thank you, thank you! I wonder what she's doing? She didn't say no, this is the house, and I'm standing here on the porch. The door's open, she knows what I'm talking about, and she's doing something about it.* Victor's mind was racing. He stood on one foot and then the other. The woman finally returned and had a smile on her lips. *That's good, that's good,* Victor encouraged himself.

"Won't you come in? My name's Colleen." She smiled
bigger now and pushed the screen door open with her right
hand, stepping aside so Victor could enter. Victor wiped his
shoes on the welcome mat, smiled at Colleen, and stepped in.

"I sure do appreciate any help at all in learning more
about Mr. Watt," Victor told her. What an understatement
that was, as he would soon find out.

The house was as striking on the inside as it was outside.
Shiny hardwood floors covered with thick, rich, deep-colored
area rugs; high wooden ceilings with ornate crown molding;
pastel-painted wood walls with many old watercolor and oil
paintings, each hanging from a thick velvet cord. Antiques
were everywhere—everywhere! Chairs, tables, lamps, books,
stools, couches...all antique. *What a showplace, what a
museum*, Victor thought.

"Please follow me," Colleen said, pleasantly.

They walked from this large atrium/sitting area through
a doorway into an old-fashioned parlor that was just as
stuffed with antiques. This room felt more snug than the
other. It had a lower ceiling and a small fireplace. The area
rug in here was of deep reds and dark blues. Sitting in a delicate fabric-and-wood armchair was an elderly woman. She
had white hair, was very thin, wore glasses that made her
blue eyes look larger than normal, and had such a sweet
smile. Victor was captivated.

"Mama, this is Mr. Victor Truman, the man I told you
about. And Mr. Truman, this is my mother, Mrs. Minnie
Nelson." Colleen spoke deliberately and slightly slower.

Victor smiled, still looking at those eyes and that sweet
smile. He made a half-bow to the mother.

"It's a pleasure to meet you, ma'am. Thank you for seeing me."

"Sit down, young man." The old woman motioned with her hand for Victor to sit in a chair like hers on the opposite side of the fireplace.

"Well, I'll leave you two to talk. Mr. Truman, may I offer you some refreshment?" Colleen awaited his response with folded hands, as if in prayer.

"Please, call me Victor. No, no thank you, I'm very comfortable." Victor looked at Minnie. "Mrs. Nelson?"

"Colleen, dear, bring us a pitcher of your delicious lemonade. That should hit the spot on a day like today."

Victor thought of the local radio program he had heard just that morning. A pitcher of lemonade sounded good.

"I'll be right back." Colleen left the room and Victor turned to face Minnie Nelson.

"Colleen tells me you asked of Clement Watt." The old woman's blue eyes sparkled. That sweet smile returned.

"Yes, Mrs. Nelson. I found this newspaper article from 1899 that says Mr. Watt stayed here when he was in town." Victor was holding the copy.

"May I see that?" she asked.

"Of course, Mrs. Nelson."

The old woman reached out her hand and Victor leaned forward to give it to her. "And don't call me Mrs. Nelson. My name's Minnie. I'm over eighty, but I don't feel eighty. 'Mrs. Nelson' makes me sound old." She winked at Victor and showed that sweet smile again.

"Yes, Minnie. And you sure don't look eighty, either."

"Oh aren't you the charmer. I'll bet you're married, aren't you?"

"Yes, ma'am—er, yes, Minnie, I am."

"Sure you are, you smooth-talker. Wouldn't take long for some sharp little gal to hook a catch like you." Oh, that smile again. Victor smiled back.

Minnie was enjoying every bit of the old article. Victor followed her eyes and could see that she was taking in every word. When she finished, her eyes jumped back to re-read the headline.

"Mr. Watt. Dear, dear Clement," she spoke, but not to Victor. Then her eyes focused on Victor. "And what would you like to know about Clement Watt?" She was serious now, with a bit of suspicion and protectiveness in her voice.

"I want to know *everything* about him," Victor said, naively.

"Why?" she questioned.

Colleen entered the room with a tray on which sat a tall glass pitcher of lemonade and two glasses filled with ice. She placed it on the small antique coffee table in front of a love seat against the wall.

"Here, I'll do the honors." Victor stood and thanked Colleen.

"Oh, isn't he the chivalrous one," Minnie teased, her playful mood returning.

Colleen giggled and said, "I see you two are getting along fine. Call me if you need anything; I'll be in the kitchen."

Victor poured out two glasses of lemonade and handed one to Minnie. He sat down again and took a sip.

"Ummm, that's good."

"Homemade from homegrown lemons," Minnie declared, and took a sip herself.

"Now why are you so interested in Clement Watt?" Minnie asked.

Victor was impressed. *This old gal doesn't miss a trick. Gets right down to business.*

"I didn't actually even know his name until yesterday, when I found that article over at the *Daily Gazette* newspaper office.

"Well, why were you looking for this article?" she pushed.

"I'll have to back up a bit," Victor explained, sitting up in his chair.

"All right, back up then. We have all day," said Minnie with mock gruffness.

"Good. Thank you, Mrs.—er, Minnie. I was hoping we didn't have to rush our conversation."

"Never rush anything, young man. You remember that. Everything—everything—has its own time, its own pace, its own rhythm, and only a fool tries to rush that. Sorry thing is, the world is full of fools." Minnie smiled again.

"Yes, ma'am."

"Now you tell me everything." She placed her glass on a side table, folded the article up, handed it back to Victor, and sat back in her arm chair as if to say "Let's have it!"

"You mean it? You mean *everything?*"

"I said 'everything,' didn't I?"

"Yes, you did. Okay, here goes...."

Victor began his autobiography and discovery of the cemetery. Minnie Nelson carefully listened to every word. She never interrupted and never showed any signs of emotion. She just listened with the sincerest, dearest look on her face, so soothing it made it very easy for Victor to tell her things about himself that he had never said to another person—not even Christine.

When he finished nearly an hour later, with "And so here I am, talking with you," Minnie remained silent and still, as if summing up everything he had just told her. Victor took a swallow of lemonade.

Then Minnie broke the long silence: "You're a seeker."

"What am I?" Victor raised his eyebrows.

"You're a seeker. And that's very, very special. I sensed this, and that's why I had Colleen invite you in. Very special, seekers are. Clement would have taken fondly to you."

Victor's expression showed he wanted to know more.

"Now let *me* do some talking." Her hands were clasped with both index fingers pressed together and pointed upward. She rested them against her lips, as if considering how to put what she was going to say next.

"I remember that cemetery well. Papa used to take us there after church on Sundays. Seems a bit odd, a cemetery for family outings, doesn't it? But it was pretty much the local custom to pass through the cemetery over to the big meadow where the townsfolk would gather on Sundays. Those are pleasant memories.

"I know the headstone you saw—Clement's. I saw it once quite some time after he passed on. I didn't know of the date he secreted in the stone's decoration, but the words he posed, Take the first step—no more, no less—and the next will be revealed, are very much Clement's. I knew he must have personally ordered those carved when I first laid eyes on them. While I never heard him speak quite those exact words, that was the principle he lived—and prospered—by. If even just a handful of us would live our lives in an attempt to completely understand that message, not only would we reach the heights we long for, but this whole world would vastly improve.

"Please, young man, Victor: Do not judge or draw any conclusions about what I'm telling you here, as difficult as it will be. Keep an open mind as best you can. You are hearing things that very, very few people ever do. I don't know why for certain, but I have a glimpse into it all because it has been revealed to me, in just the way those carved words you've seen promise.

"Clement Watt was a wise man, a very special, very wise man. Not in the way you think I mean, and not in the way this foolish world thinks. He was wiser than the world. I never thought about it that way before now, but he was wiser than this world we live in."

Minnie paused and Victor started to speak. She stopped him by holding up an index finger.

"I was just into my thirties, and had just borne Colleen when Clement passed on. Before that, there's no time in my life that I don't remember him. My mama—that's Emma— and papa ran a little boarding house right here, on this property. It was good for us all. The whole family would pitch in and help with all the chores and extra work that the guests required. Our boarders enjoyed being part of a real family as well. Oh, some would just stay a short while and then leave a little huffy, sayin' it was too much comin's and goin's and not enough peace and quiet. 'Good riddin's!' Papa used to say about 'em. 'If they don't like this family and what we got here, then they can just go to—,' well, you know."

Victor smiled.

"Poor old Papa; he had such a temper. Anyhow, there's never a time I don't recall that Clement wasn't boarding with us. Whenever he was here, which seemed to be at least a few days every month, sometimes longer, I remember him being in the garden. He loved the garden. We always had the prettiest garden in the neighborhood, and I do suspect it was on account of Clement.

"I remember one summer evening: It was hot, oh it was hot. It was just about my bedtime, but I so wanted to stay up and sit with the grown-ups on our front porch. There was Papa and Mama, my uncle Charley, and Clement. I knew exactly what I was doing when I went outside on the porch and, with my sweetest little voice, rolling my big blue eyes, asked if they'd like me to make them up another pitcher of lemonade before I went off to bed. I think they knew what I was up to and said yes, that would be real nice. So I hurried into the kitchen, squeezed those lemons, and brought back a big fresh pitcher of lemonade. And then I just sat down next to Clement and didn't leave. I'm certain they noticed, but no one said anything and I had the time of my life, sitting up late with the grown-ups, listening to their voices muffled by the night, trailing off the porch into the darkness where the crickets took over.

"At one point Papa said he couldn't figure out why we weren't always full up, that we always had a room or two that went empty. He said he reckoned we had the cleanest, tidiest house and the best home cookin' this side of the Mississippi, then I saw him nudge Mama and make her giggle and blush. 'And on top of all that, we got the prettiest darn garden in town!' he said, givin' Clement a jab on the knee. 'We're doin' everything right, so what's wrong?' I remember him asking.

"Clement said, 'W. J.,' that's what everyone called Papa, 'you know how many eggs a codfish lays at one time?' Papa looked at Clement like he just took leave of his senses.

"'No, Clement, I reckon I don't. How many?'

"'A million,' Clement told him. Papa made a surprised face. 'And how many eggs does an old hen lay at one time?'

"'Just one,' Papa answered. I could tell Papa knew Clement wasn't just jokin' now.

"'That's right, just one. And what does the codfish do after she lays those one million eggs?'

"'Well, I don't know,' Papa said, 'what does she do?'

"'Nothing. She does nothing after laying one million eggs. But what does that old hen do after she lays just that one egg?'

"'She cackles up a storm!' Papa was catching on, but he still couldn't quite see the point of this.

"'That's exactly right: she cackles. So what does that tell you, W. J.?' Papa couldn't think of anything to say. 'It tells you that it pays to advertise!'

"I remember they all burst into laughter—even Mama— but then she shushed them, saying we were going to wake our boarders and the neighbors.

"'So what are you saying exactly, Clement?' Papa asked.

"'I'm saying to toot your own horn and ring your own bell. Take out an advertisement and tell people how good your place is here. In fact, tell 'em you're so picky and particular that you take applications and require references before you'll let just anybody board at Emma's!'

"Papa put an advertisement in the paper like that. It worked magic, and we always had a waiting list of people wanting to board with us. That's when we built this house that you're in now, with three times the number of rooms, that were always full up. Still would be to this day, but Colleen and her husband and children just like it nice and manageable now without having to bring in outside help to tend to so many boarders like we used to do.

"I remember Papa and Clement talking business around the kitchen table late one night when I got out of bed for water. I always figured that Clement helped Papa with the money. That's when he had his own private room that was always his whether he was here or not—and mostly he was not."

Victor couldn't resist: "He lived right here, in this very house?"

"Just above our heads here." She pointed to the ceiling. "That was his favorite room, with a balcony and clear view out over the park across the street.

"Clement was a wise man; he understood things the rest of us didn't. Like I said, he was wiser than this world. When he was here, I could actually feel a change in the atmosphere. I can't describe this very well, but I'll try:

"We never knew when Clement would be here, but like I said, usually a month never went by that he didn't spend three or four days with us. It was never regular; we just never knew. Everyone was fond of Clement—especially me—and his visit was always a pleasant surprise we looked forward to.

"Usually I would find him here when I came home from school, but before I set foot on the front porch, I knew that he was here. He brought a peacefulness with him wherever he went. He was a quiet man—I never saw him emotional—but he was not shy at all."

Minnie gave that smile again, closed her eyes, laughed, and continued. "I always thought of him as a lion: He was never mean, but nothing swayed him. He could walk into any kind of situation and knew precisely what to do. Confidence, complete confidence, that's what he had."

"What did he look like?" Victor interrupted again, but Minnie didn't seem to mind.

"He's right here among us," Minnie smiled. Victor felt a rush of goose bumps sweep over his back. She pointed and looked to the back wall of the parlor. A portrait hung in a simple gold-leafed wooden frame from a black velvet cord.

"That's him?" Victor stood and walked over to the picture. A large family Bible lay atop a waist-high antique wood bookstand directly beneath the picture. Victor had to lean over it to get close enough to read the small, white, handmade letters in the lower right corner. "Matthew Brady Studios, New York, 1892? This is a Matthew Brady photograph?"

"That process was called daguerreotype. It's a copper plate. I remember as a small girl begging Clement for a picture of himself so he could be around even when he wasn't here." Minnie chuckled. "I do believe it took over a year of my asking before he brought me that. He said it was taken when he was forty years old, so by the time he brought it to me, some twenty years had passed." She chuckled again.

"Did it look like him?" Victor asked, seriously.

Minnie was laughing now. "Not very much. When he presented that to me, I was just a young girl, as I said, and usually wasn't too tactful. I said, 'Who is this? I asked for a picture of *you*,' and Clement and I just laughed and laughed. Mama found out later what I had said and was so embarrassed of her improper little girl. I remember she turned red, opened her mouth, and placed her hands against her cheeks, aghast that I could be so rude. But Clement just laughed. He couldn't have cared less. That man had no vanity in his bones."

Victor was laughing along with Minnie when he sat down again.

"It's getting rather warm," Minnie said, fanning her face with her hand.

Oh no, don't make me leave now, Victor thought, *not yet.*

"Would you care to escort me to the verandah where it's a bit cooler?" Minnie raised her elbow for Victor to help her up. They walked arm in arm out through the foyer, through the front door, and onto the broad, shady front porch.

"Now which is your favorite chair?" Victor asked.

"I have a fondness for that rocking chair just over there." She nodded her head toward the end of the porch, right under the cupola.

"Then that's where we're going." Victor smiled.

Their footsteps sounded good on the wooden floor. Victor helped her into the old rocking chair.

"I'll go get our lemonade," he said.

Colleen must have heard them walking and leaned out the front door.

"Can I get you two anything?"

"Yes, Colleen. How about some of your delicious mint iced tea now? That will ward off this heat."

"Good idea, mama. It'll take a few minutes, but I'll be back." Colleen disappeared into the kitchen.

"You sit right there." Minnie pointed to the swing seat. "This is how Clement and I used to sit and talk after supper. I sat where you are, and he'd sit in this rocking chair."

Victor raised his eyebrows. "*That* rocking chair?"

"This very chair." Minnie smiled her smile and closed her eyes for one brief moment. Victor smiled, too, his eyes trailing off across the street to the park.

"The most valuable times of my life were spent right here on this porch with Clement." She continued with what she wanted to impart to Victor, who sat up in the swing, eager for his lesson to continue.

"Mr. Clement Watt was a wealthy man. He was a spectacularly wealthy and powerful man. But more than just in the way you're thinking, and not in the way the world wants to think upon these things."

Victor cocked his head to the side the way a puppy does when it's trying to understand.

"Clement Watt owned more companies and more railroads and more businesses and more land than anyone—including myself—ever knew. He used those things as part of a pure, higher purpose: to show others the fallacy of the world's ways. He used his vast wealth and position to teach. Yes, Clement was a teacher. He would have been infinitely more contented, I think, being a gardener. But then who would have listened, and who would have cared? That's the way this world is. But he wasn't after the masses, either. With his extreme wealth and power, he could have commanded the front page of newspapers whenever he desired. He could have reached the masses with the wave of his little finger. No, Clement was looking for seekers, like yourself.

"He dealt with the world's most powerful men—presidents and leaders. I once heard a rumor around town here that Clement had just come from a meeting at the White House with President Woodrow Wilson, so I asked him about it—if the rumor was true. We were sitting right out here as I recollect. Clement smiled at me and said, 'Minnie, would you think any less of me if I *didn't* have dinner with the President?'

"I took that to mean that he had indeed just seen President Wilson, because I never mentioned the rumor saying anything about him having *dinner* with the President." She winked and smiled at Victor. He chuckled and thought how rambunctious she must have been as a young woman.

"I know for a fact that Clement saw Warren Harding quite often, and they would exchange cigars. And Mark Twain, too; he and Clement got along famously and enjoyed each other's company—and cigars.

"Gee, that's surprising…" Victor thought aloud.

"Why?" asked Minnie.

"Well, you'd think that someone so special—so wise— wouldn't have a bad habit like that."

"There you go thinkin' again!" Minnie sat up a little straighter, and Victor knew another lesson was coming. "First of all, nothing smells quite so good as the aroma from a fine, handmade cigar. It's those cheap, stinky ones nowadays that give cigars a bad reputation."

Victor smiled. It seemed funny, this cute little woman praising a good cigar.

"Some of the fondest memories I have are those times when I'd get a whiff of one of Clement's cigars halfway down the block walking home from school. I'd smile with delight and run the rest of the way home, knowing I'd find Clement tending the garden.

"Other times, on hot summer nights, my papa and Clement would be sittin', talkin' softly on the front porch, and the rich, woodsy scent of Clement's cigar would find its way up to my room. I used to love that; it made me feel as if I was down on the porch with them. It made me feel connected to them."

Victor understood, and felt grateful that Minnie was shar- ing these special moments with him.

"When I would make a generalized, ignorant—" Minnie winked at Victor, "—statement as you just did about cigars,

Clement would quote Shakespeare, from Hamlet: 'There is nothing either good or bad, but thinking makes it so.'"

Victor nodded, as he contemplated what Minnie had just said.

"When you *watch* your thoughts, Victor, instead of being taken over by them, you have an open mind, which is the way it should be. Then—and only then—can you *receive* the answers you desire. Another of Clement's favorite truisms came from the Bible, I believe: 'Nothing is secret, that shall not be made manifest.' Even down to cigars."

Minnie paused and smiled at Victor. "And about your comment regarding something being a 'bad habit': The world has this all backwards as well. Another passage, from Matthew, wisely teaches that it's 'Not that which goeth into the mouth defileth a man; but that which cometh out of the mouth, this defileth a man.' The more you remember to watch your thoughts, the clearer you will see the truth in this, Victor. While the world wastes its life on curing 'bad habits,' you work at watching your thoughts. As you do that, all else will take care of itself."

Victor felt the depth of wisdom in this. He didn't comprehend it fully, but he sensed that it was true, and that his life would take on an entirely new meaning and focus as a result of this visit with Minnie.

"I believe Clement knew that he could help more people by helping those who were, in turn, overseers of many more people. He once said that a drop of water at the source of a river was imbued with much more responsibility and potential than a water drop down at the mouth of the river."

"What was he trying to help people do?" Victor asked.

"He tried to convey to people that there is a higher level to life, and that it is completely possible to live it right here and now."

"But he owned so much, and carried such weight…why would he spend his time when the world isn't interested?"

"For the few who seek, for those fortunate few of us who have that tiny spark in us and desire a better life that we sense is possible. Clement was a living example that such a life is possible—and completely practical. He used to read Shakespeare, Walden, Thoreau, Balzac, Longfellow—he was very fond of Longfellow—and other classic literature and say, 'If people only knew the lessons these writers teach! The baker, the clerk, the minister, the schoolboy, the banker, and the school marm could all be happy and prosperous.' He published a little book that he made sure every one of his hundreds of employees received. He called it *Something You Should Know*. He planted that seed in every one of them; and in many, it took root. Anyone who worked for Clement was very fortunate indeed.

"To have the wisdom that he had carries a certain responsibility—and the desire—to share it with other like-minded individuals."

Minnie repositioned herself in her chair as she thought of an example. "Suppose you were coming out of a jungle that you had tried for years to get through. After so much effort, you discovered that taking the treacherous jungle path not only led nowhere, but was unnecessary as well. Finally leaving the jungle once and for always, you see hoards of people running to get through the jungle that you just discovered the secret of. Now I ask you, Victor, would you tell them?" Minnie leaned forward, those big blue eyes open wide, awaiting Victor's response.

"Yes, of course I would."

"But what if only one or two of those people at a time heeded your admonitions?" She leaned back, eyes still wide.

"I would still try."

"Then you know the answer to your question. With the wisdom that Clement possessed comes a certain responsibility—and joy—to tell others."

CHAPTER 7

Victor was trying to absorb the big mental mouthful of information that Minnie had revealed to him, but a thousand questions were cropping up at the same time.

"Well, what did he understand about the jungle exactly?" he finally asked. It seemed that Minnie had just answered that, but something still wasn't registering about her metaphor. He hoped she didn't consider him inane and a disappointment. Minnie smiled knowingly. *Good*, Victor thought.

"I'm going to tell you something of what Clement Watt knew. This isn't to say that you'll now know it simply because I speak it to you. This is just the first step that places you closer to the edge of the jungle."

Victor thought of the words inscribed in Clement Watt's headstone.

"You can then begin to see your way clear of the jungle, or you can run right back in it—as dangerous and painful as it is—as most people do, preferring the known over the unknown." Victor felt the gravity of what was coming.

"What I'm about to tell you, Victor, will shock you. We don't have the luxury of time, you and I, and this is a fortuitous opportunity for a very special seed to be planted in your care. Like the parable of the sower, some seeds fell beside the road and birds came and ate them; others fell on rocky places; and some fell among thorns. But a few fell on good soil and yielded a crop, some a hundredfold, some sixty, and some thirty. And by the way, Victor, that chapter goes on to say that for whoever has, *more* shall be given and he shall have an abundance; but whoever does not have, even what he has shall be taken away from him."

"Do you mean the rich get richer and the poor get poorer?" Victor pondered.

"Yes," she said pointing a finger, "but not in the way you're thinking. Victor! Stop thinking about money! Money—and the wise use of it—comes with understanding. The wise are rich, and more just naturally comes, including money, if that's their desire. The foolish are poor, and blessings—including money—naturally elude them. Don't pursue money, Victor. Seek understanding first, then all things just naturally follow. Do you see why the world is foolish?"

Victor nodded.

Colleen came out onto the porch, the screen door slapping closed behind her. "Here's that special order: A full pitcher of my secret-recipe mint iced tea." She set a fresh tray of one large pitcher, two glasses of ice, a small plate of cookies, and napkins down on a round wicker side table between Victor and Minnie.

Just then a blue jay landed on the porch railing, looked directly at Minnie, and began yapping and chattering up a storm. Minnie feigned surprise and then shooed him away with her hand. "Git! Git! You old jabber mouth, git! I'll talk to you later. Can't you see I have company today? Git!" She looked at Victor with a hopeless expression. Victor began laughing. Colleen giggled and went back into the house.

They were alone again. It was warm and still outside. Big, white, puffy clouds dangled in the sky. A slight breeze moved only the leaves of the trees; it wasn't quite strong enough to cool things down. Victor and Minnie sat and sipped Colleen's sweet, delicious iced tea, taking in the immense quiet. Their gazes met and they conducted a silent, mental conversation:

Do you sincerely wish to know The Secret?

Yes, Minnie, please tell me.

She began as if that conversation had been spoken aloud. "All right, then. The Secret is this: There is something enormously wrong with how we think; how *you* think, how *I* think, how *everyone* thinks. I can't explain it, and I don't understand it to any great degree. But I can tell you what to do about it. This is what Clement Watt's life's work was all about. It's what all of the wise men who ever walked this earth tried to teach others."

Victor never expected to hear anything like this, especially not from a sweet little eighty-year-old woman. But he sensed that what she had just told him was true. Absolutely true. He took a deep breath and was expressionless, his eyes fixed on the floor. He took another deep breath and looked up at Minnie. She was watching him closely and knew it was time to continue.

"Victor, look at all those trees." She made a sweeping motion with her thin, wrinkled arm and hand. "Do they fight amongst themselves, resent each other, and say to themselves, 'I should be a pine tree instead of a magnolia'?"

Victor smiled and moved his head back and forth slightly, looking.

"Do they fret about the heat today, or worry about what tomorrow will bring, or moan about what happened to them yesterday? No. Well, then, why aren't you and I as happy, carefree, and *successful* as these trees? Because our brains are more sophisticated than the tiny brains these trees have."

Victor enjoyed her one-sided question-and-answer monologue. He thought Minnie should have been a school teacher, for she would have been a good one. Who knows? Perhaps she had been.

Minnie leaned forward and downward, her eyes looking up to Victor now. She lowered her voice but increased its intensity. "Victor Truman," she said—he felt like a kid in the principal's office—"I'm about to divulge to you something that very, *very* few people ever learn. And that's the operative word: Learn. You must now seek to learn and understand what I'm about to tell you. There is nothing in this life more important to seek than the understanding of this. *Nothing.* 'Seek ye first the kingdom of Heaven and *all things* shall be added unto you' is how it's been so eloquently put."

Victor straightened himself.

"Those thoughts that rush through your mind, my mind, Clement's mind, Plato's mind, everyone's mind, are not ours. We do not create them; they come from somewhere outside us. Not knowing—or even suspecting—this, we take them to be our own individual, self-made thoughts. We believe we *are* these thoughts." Victor didn't know what to say, but before he could decide, she continued.

"What's wrong with believing that we create them is that we carry these horrendous thoughts—this beast—around at all times believing that we are it!"

This was a lot for Victor to take in all at once and Minnie could see this. She sat back in her chair, took a sip of iced tea, and gave Victor that understanding, motherly look. He returned a weak smile.

"Now look, Victor," she continued in a softer, calmer voice. "There is only one thing on this earth to understand, and it is what I just told you. Seeking, not even resolving, but simply *seeking* to understand this fact that we are not our thoughts will answer any and every question you will ever pose. This is not philosophy, Victor; it is rock-solid, practical living." She pushed the back of one hand into the open palm of the other. It made a slight smacking sound. "You don't know what to do with your life? *This* is what to do with it. Study *this*, and you'll always get your right answer.

"Have you read *Dr. Jekyll and Mr. Hyde?*"

"No, I haven't read it." Victor hoped she wouldn't scold him.

"Read it, Victor!" Minnie smiled. "It's a story of what we're speaking about! Clement spoke of that book very often. He dined privately with Robert Louis Stevenson on several occasions and told me fascinating accounts of their conversations."

Victor was feeling overwhelmed now. "So what do I *do* about these thoughts you speak of? I *have* to think!" he said somewhat desperately.

Minnie smiled compassionately. "Yes, dear, you do—we all do. But you must begin to think in a new way; you must begin to think *differently* than you do now. How? It's the most simple, yet most profound, idea you have ever heard: You must begin to watch your thoughts." Minnie paused and smiled. She looked angelic, eyes shining, her two small hands, resting one on the other, in her lap.

"But I know what I'm thinking," Victor responded, with doubt.

"Victor, do you know that you have the most worried look on your face now, that it's wrinkled like a prune? And do you know that your right leg is beating faster than a humming-bird's wings?"

Victor froze, his eyes fixed for a moment. He looked down and caught his right leg bouncing madly against the seat. He stopped his leg, closed his eyes, relaxed his face, and looked sheepishly at Minnie. Then they both smiled at one another.

"That is what Clement used to call being lost in thought. And that type of hypnosis is how most people live their entire lives. That hypnosis, and abiding by what the beast in our head constantly tells us, is how this poor world operates. Wars, fights, lawsuits, neighbor-against-neighbor, crime, fear, and anxiety are a result of listening to those beastly thoughts and believing we are them.

"Shakespeare said 'Sleep no more!' This is what he meant by that. This hypnosis that we're under keeps us forever running in circles, like the donkey chasing a carrot."

"But all this great literature you mentioned that addresses this secret, how come none of its millions and millions of readers gets the message?" Victor's eyes narrowed, awaiting her response.

"That is a perfect demonstration of how insidious this entire thought process is, Victor. It's so well-veiled. Tell me, have you read any of the literature I spoke of?"

"Yes, some of it."

"And what did you think?"

"I thought it was cumbersome reading, so much before my time that I missed most of its original meaning."

"And did your professors help?" She raised her eyebrows.

"Well, they taught us that these people in the story had the same fears, desires, and problems that we have today, in modern times."

"So what did you infer from the observation?"

"That nothing's changed."

"And that you're just pretty much normal the way you are, and that life's a struggle," she finished his sentence.

"Right," Victor nodded.

"We take it as history, as entertainment. We don't see the obvious. Clement mentioned *The Purloined Letter* to me once, by Edgar Allan Poe, whom he said he would have enjoyed meeting. I read it, and he and I discussed it in the garden one day.

"'We don't see the obvious,' he said, is the lesson in that story. Our thoughts are as close as our own breath, but we never take a close look at them! I imagine I had likely asked him the same question you just asked of me."

"We don't see the obvious," Victor repeated, half to himself.

"Another of his favorite people and authors was Walt Whitman. He and Clement apparently spent much time together. I remember being the center of attention among my little classmates at school, reveling in telling stories about conversations that Clement and Mr. Whitman had had. My teacher, I remember, once accused me of fabricating fanciful tales. I was so upset by this, and ran the whole way home that day to tell Clement how abominably I had been treated, and how humiliated I was." Minnie made a sorrowful face to demonstrate how she looked that day many years ago, and then smiled. Victor chuckled.

"I came running into the backyard here," Minnie pointed her thumb behind her, "and found Clement where he usually was—working in the garden, on his hands and knees, enjoying one of his big cigars. I blurted out my tale of woe to him and he raised up on one knee. He put his hands on my shoulders and looked me straight in the eyes with that wonderful, knowing expression of his.

"'Minnie,' he said softly and calmly, 'now what told you to get so upset and flustered like this?'

"'Just a thought in my head,' I replied, hanging my head, knowing I had forgotten again." Minnie took a deep breath and exhaled. "Oh, that dear, kind man was so patient with me.

"'And what did that thought tell you exactly?' he continued.

"'It told me that I was ugly—uglier than all the other girls—and that I didn't deserve to have an important friend like you, and that I wanted them to like me.'"

Victor had a sad look on his face, listening to Minnie recall this memory.

"Victor, wake up!" she snapped, clapping her hands. Victor was startled. "Don't you go getting lost in thought over this. Stay awake now! Know that you're sitting here with me on this porch. Sense where your feet are. Know if your hands are tight or relaxed. If you don't know these things, you're hypnotized, asleep, and those thoughts took you over again."

With a smile barely breaking past her lips, Minnie barked these orders in the sternest manner she could muster. Victor pictured her as a military drill instructor and smiled. "Come on, come awake," she motioned with her hand to do what she had said.

Separating himself mentally, as if thinking outside of himself, he saw that his face was tight and wrinkled around his eyes. Then he sensed his rigid jaw and relaxed it. His hands were clenched, and he opened them. His toes were tightly curled; he let them loose. Then he noticed his shoulders were bunched up, and he let them relax. Then he looked at Minnie.

"That'a boy," she smiled, reassuringly. "If you don't know where you are, you're lost in thought. And if you're asleep like that, those thoughts have a fine ole time running you ragged." She lifted her chin and gave one nod of her head downward as if to add an exclamation point to the end of that statement. She smiled and said, "Now where was I before you went to sleep on me?"

Victor couldn't remember, and just as he began to feel ashamed, he caught it: Once again he removed himself from himself and quickly did a rundown on his condition—face, jaw, hands, feet, shoulders. He also noticed he was breathing in short breaths. He took in a deep breath and let his body relax as he exhaled.

Minnie noticed all this with great approval on her face. "That's right!" She winked at Victor. "Clement pointed to a rosebush among all the others there in the corner of the back-yard..."

Victor's mind started to wander off to the radio talk show he listened to last evening. But then he caught his wandering mind and came back again. He didn't think Minnie noticed.

"…and said, 'Minnie, what if all these other rosebushes suddenly didn't like this one rosebush here? Would that make any difference at all to this rosebush?'

"'No," I answered.

"'And would this one rosebush be any less spectacular than it is now?'

"'No,' I said again.

"'Then what is the *only* thing that could make this little rosebush here feel sad and hurt?' he asked me.

"'Only if the little rosebush had thoughts about the other rosebushes.'

"'That's absolutely right. And what if this little rosebush *even did* have those hurtful thoughts, what could it do?'

"'It could know that they were there, but it wouldn't have to listen to them!' Clement smiled and gave my shoulders a little squeeze with both hands.

"'That's right, Minnie!' he said."

Victor was amazed how Minnie could remember those conversations so precisely.

"Victor," Minnie continued, "you always remember this, what you've learned here today: There's nothing to do, there's only something to see. Just be the unbiased observer in your life, and everything you'll ever need to know will be revealed and given to you. Clement used to say this to me when I'd fire off a barrage of questions, 'Well, what about this and what about that…'" she tapped her fingers and thumb together rapidly, imitating a bird's beak. Then she chuckled. "I must have sounded like that old blue jay. Come to think on it, that's what my mind sounds like!"

Victor nodded, realizing how insightful her little joke was.

"But the important thing is to *know* that our minds are doing this, Victor. Not that you're to fight those thoughts, or try to suppress them, or even try to drown them out—we can't anyway. You just remember to watch them. Watch and watch and watch. And then, watch what happens!" There was that special smile again.

Colleen poked her head through the doorway again. "Mama, it's time for your nap now."

"Oh, I'm too wound up to rest," Minnie raised her arms, "but Colleen's right, I should go lie down."

"Minnie, how will I ever thank you?" Victor breathed deeply and looked at the frail, sweet old woman.

"By stayin' awake and makin' the best use of your life!" she said with forced sternness. Clement used to tell me 'Life isn't a foot race, Minnie, it's just a great big classroom to learn in.'"

"It just seems so overwhelming. Almost impossible."

"Colleen?" Minnie looked to her left to see if Colleen was still standing in the doorway. She was. "Bring that family Bible out here to our friend." She turned to Victor with a look that said "Wait until you see *this*."

Colleen returned to the porch carrying the large, thick Bible and carefully placed it on Victor's lap. It was heavy. The cover was gold-stamped, and had beautiful gold-edged pages. It looked very old and had been read often.

Victor looked up at Minnie with a smile.

"Open it," she ordered expectantly, waving a hand.

Victor placed his right hand along the edge of the smooth gold pages and felt a separation. He carefully opened the Bible at that place and let the top half open out fully and rest on his

left thigh. He looked down on the open Bible and a chill coursed over him from his scalp to his toes.

"This is—I don't believe it—this is *impossible*!" His mouth was open and his eyes were wide.

"Yep, so impossible that you're looking right at it," Minnie said matter-of-factly.

There in front of him—fragile, flat, and wrinkled—was a sky-blue rose carefully dried between the pages of the Bible.

"This is impossible!" he repeated, mouth and eyes still open. "I don't believe this! I just heard an expert on roses—an *expert*—say that a sky-blue rose is an impossibility, that it can't be done!" He stared at the blue rose.

Minnie chuckled, her eyes twinkling again. "That's what the world tells you. 'It's impossible,' they say. All the experts, Victor, believe those harmful thoughts in their heads. But you know different now; you know better. Now see what Clement had to say to those so-called experts." She motioned to the Bible again.

Victor looked down, still amazed, and saw a piece of yellowed stationery resting on the pages to the left, opposite the blue rose. At the top center of the sheet, two letters in old-fashioned type were printed: C. W. There was handwriting in old black fountain-pen ink. Victor looked up at Minnie, eyebrows raised. She smiled.

"He wrote this?" Victor looked back down at the paper and read aloud:

> Things are not what they seem.
> Always seek "The Impossible," which is
> never more than a step away.

The chill surged through Victor's body.

"Nothing is impossible, my dear Victor, as long as you remember to leave those thoughts and just watch them go by. Never flinch; just watch." She remembered something and continued. "Once I said in exasperation to Clement, 'I just don't know how to not listen to those awful thoughts in my head, I just don't know how!' and Clement smiled at me and said, 'Now is how, Minnie. Always, remember now and the how comes of its own, almost magically.'"

Victor looked down at the blue rose and the handwriting again. A peaceful feeling came over him.

"Does anyone know about this blue rose, Minnie?"

"Just my family. And now you, of course," she added.

"You never told anyone about it?"

"Oh, I wanted to tell everyone, to tell the world, in fact, but I know better now."

"But the world's been trying to create a blue rose for…forever. I just heard that expert on the radio last night say the Japanese and Australians are conducting expensive experiments—splitting genes—trying desperately to create one of these." Victor looked down and studied the blue rose again.

"I know, I know, Victor." She held her hand up, her palm facing him. "This is quite a gardening community, and we would have become immensely famous having a blue rose growing in our garden. The American Rose Society would have named it after Clement. It would have made the cover of *The Saturday Evening Post* magazine even."

"Well, what happened?" Victor couldn't wait to hear the rest of the story. And he had so many more questions.

"This was one of the last times Clement was here—just two or three months before he passed on. I was married by then, and we all lived together in this very house. Clement had a corner of the backyard that was just his, for his small garden. Papa had built him his own potting and tool shed.

"When he was here, other than the brief walks he would make over to the courthouse and bank and such, Clement was usually in his garden. He loved those flowers.

"I was across the yard putting clothes on the line and Clement called me over. Like I said, this is quite a gardening town, and I knew what I was seeing. I couldn't believe my eyes—just like you—but there it was: that pretty true-blue rose, just one of many centifolias—what we called Cabbage roses—on a rather tall plant. Every other rose on that plant was what it was supposed to be—what was called the Paul Neyron variety first introduced way back in 1869. They all were as usual, a deep pink, with row upon row of petals. But there, right in front of me, was the one blue one. And like you, Victor, I said those exact words: 'This is impossible!'"

Victor started to interrupt. Minnie knew his question and kept talking.

"I looked at it and touched it carefully to see if Clement wasn't playing a trick on me. Then I asked him how it happened: Was it a cutting, did he bud it, was it hybridized?

"Clement just laughed at all my carryin' on. Then he asked, 'Minnie, you want to know *how?*' And I finished his lesson with 'I know: *Now* is how.' 'That's right,' he said, 'Why can't we just stand here and enjoy this beautiful expression of nature? Why would we want to let the foolish world in on our special little secret? It surely wouldn't be special after that.'

"I came out in the yard every day—sometimes several times a day—to admire that beautiful, one-of-a-kind rose. When it reached its full bloom, I begged Clement to let me pluck it and press it in that family Bible. He reluctantly agreed."

"I'm sure glad he did," Victor whispered, still wondering how it could have happened. Minnie saw the wheels turning in his head.

"Victor, you're still trying to figure it out, aren't you? Your mind is scrambling to explain it, thinking perhaps the blue rose was a mutation or some such thing."

Victor smiled sheepishly.

"Well, let me tell you: I did the very same thing. Poor Clement! I came up with this theory and that, and finally he said to me, 'Minnie, don't *think*, *realize*.' I asked what he meant, and this is what he said: 'If you misspell a word over and over, you look at it, you wonder if you got it right this time, it bothers you. But then you go to the dictionary, look at it, know that it's spelled right, and from then on whenever you write that word, you don't have to *think* about it, you just *realize* it.'"

Victor paused and looked at her before he spoke. "Minnie, did that rosebush bloom again after Clement passed away?"

"My family talked and wondered about that often after Clement left us. And the very next season there were seven beautiful true-blue roses on that plant amongst the deep-pink ones."

Victor's eyes burst open. "What did you do with them? How could you keep it a secret?"

Minnie smiled and paused. "It wasn't easy. More than anyone, I knew what Clement had taught me, and I knew what the right thing to do was. I do believe Clement could have planned it all that way just to teach me. It was very diffi-cult to leave those roses on the bush and let them come and go naturally. It was very difficult. I had to work extra hard at watching those selfish, impish, greedy thoughts and not act on them. And I worked just as hard at helping my family with this too; you can imagine. But when we watched that last petal of the last of the seven blue roses die and fall away, we all knew we had done the right thing. No amount of worldly gain we could have possibly received from those roses would have come even close to the value we all received in wisdom from them."

Victor wished he fully understood what Minnie was saying.

"Clement was a truly rare and remarkable man, Victor, and he gave his whole life to let others know they can be the same."

"Did it ever bloom again?"

"No, never again—not blue or pink."

"Mama, time for that nap." Colleen must have left after she handed Victor the Bible, but she was back again, and Victor realized this was it.

"Minnie," he sounded solemn, "How can I ever thank you?"

"How? *Now* is how," she smiled, sitting forward in her rocking chair. She looked small and fragile, like the rose. Victor carefully closed the Bible and asked, "May I return this for you?"

"Oh, nonsense. Colleen and I will take care of that." She waved her hand.

"I wonder if I should keep pursuing Clement's clues—he must have meant that headstone to lead to something." Victor was puzzled.

"I'm sure he did. He certainly didn't figure on you running into me, so I can't be his secret." They laughed together.

"But you are, Minnie; you're a gold mine and a diamond all rolled into one!"

"Oh, go on," Minnie waved him away. "What does your heart—not your head—tell you to do?" she asked, touching her own heart with her fingertips.

"It tells me to keep looking," Victor said, sitting up straight. He remembered to separate himself from his thoughts. He did a quick once-over of his face, jaw, hands, feet, shoulders, and breathing. Minnie noticed and smiled.

"Then off you go, young man," she said in a motherly way.

Victor knew now that this really was good-bye.

"Minnie, may I kiss you on the cheek?" Victor surprised himself by asking this and hoped she wouldn't be offended.

"It's okay by me, but what will your sassy little wife say about it?" Minnie snapped back.

"I won't tell her, so she'll never know." Victor stood and stepped over to Minnie. She looked so sweet sitting there, like a precious little bird. He bowed down and kissed her right cheek. It made a little smack.

"My, my!" Minnie smiled, touching her cheek. "I won't wash it for a week!" she giggled.

Colleen was smiling as she stepped over and helped her mother up.

"May I help?" Victor moved to take Minnie by the arm.

"Oh, no! No! You git! You have things to go learn now." That was an interesting way to put it.

"How did you know my wife is sassy?" Victor asked.

She responded as if that were a silly question: "She has to be; didn't she *choose* to marry a seeker?" Minnie gave Victor a wink.

Victor smiled, thanked them both, picked up his white paper bag, and descended the many porch steps. He slowly walked down the wide pathway to the sidewalk. Stopping there, he turned around to watch Minnie and Colleen disappear into the house. The screen door slapped shut and Victor was alone again.

Take the first step, he thought, *and the next will be revealed. Absolutely true!* He had stepped right into a miracle.

CHAPTER 8

I'm hungry, Victor thought. *It must be close to noon. Looks like more houses from here on down the block. Think I'll go back to the Park Hotel, eat, and ask around about the orphanage.* His mind raced, and he caught it racing. It told him to hurry up. *But why?* He deliberately slowed his pace and felt each step he made. Now the thoughts *really* raced. He laughed out loud. How different this was.

As he approached Third Avenue, one block from the hotel, Victor could see that the little town had come more to life than when he had left it this morning. The people he saw were more of a local class than tourists. They were all across town in the Main Street section where he had first entered. Victor realized he didn't think of himself as a tourist any longer. He was a "local" now. Thinking of that made him smile.

Victor felt the new spring in his step as he crossed the boardwalk under Parker's General Merchandise's looming front porch. His footsteps echoed under here. *If I were wearing those goofy-looking sports shoes all the tourists wear, I wouldn't have this simple pleasure of hearing leather soles and heels clopping against this boardwalk.* Victor caught that thought. He realized how critical he was and grimaced.

"Never flinch, Victor!" He could hear Minnie's voice again. *Never flinch*, he considered, *just watch. Be an unbiased observer.*

Here's the hotel. I wonder if Walton's still here? Yes, I'll bet he is.

Victor entered the Park Hotel lobby. It was still just as grand in full daylight. Several people were passing through. And there was Walton on the phone, being his impeccable self. It felt good to see a familiar face. The big clock showed it was 12:15.

I wonder if there's a crowd in the dining room? Victor thought as he turned to exit the lobby through the archway. He walked to the podium where a young hostess in her twenties stood. As a "local," he requested "his" table-for-two in the front window. She turned, peeked around the heavy velvet curtains, turned back, smiled, picked up a menu and said, "Right this way, please."

There were more people than he'd seen on his two previous visits to the hotel dining room. Twenty, maybe thirty, were having lunch here today. Being mostly locals, he guessed they were talking business. The noise level was also higher than it was this morning at breakfast—only about four hours ago, it dawned on him—and at dinner last night. So much had happened here in such a few short hours.

Waiting for his food to be prepared, Victor read his copy of the article again. And again. "Don't *think, realize*." He remembered Clement Watt's instructions to Minnie. *All right, Clement Watt left a permanent clue—August 4, 1899—on his headstone. That led to the only record he knew that would report what happened that day: the newspaper. And that revealed this article.* Victor looked the copy over again. But what if Mr. Jessup hadn't purchased that microfiche machine? Seemed like a weak link if Mr. Watt wanted to leave a permanent chain attached to his secret.

Okay, so the next step must be in this article, and that seems obvious, really.

"Excuse me," Victor said to a passing waitress.

The waitress turned and said, "Yes, sir." That made him sound old.

"Do you know where the Children's Home—the orphanage—is from here?" She paused momentarily, her eyes rolling up to the ceiling. Victor remembered a teacher of his in the fifth grade—old Mr. Woods—catching him looking up like this when asked a question in front of the class and saying, "Is the answer written on the ceiling, Victor?" The whole class laughed.

"Yes," the waitress continued, "go out the hotel, turn left to the corner, turn left on Second Avenue, go down three blocks to Watt Street, turn left again and go another block. You'll see it standing all by itself. It takes in the whole block. It's a very large, two-story, white building all by itself." She smiled, realizing that was a lot to memorize after all.

Victor repeated it to her and traced an invisible route in the air in front of him. He thought this must look very strange to anyone watching from another table. The waitress smiled and nodded that he understood her directions.

"Got it. Thanks," he said. "Watt Street," he whispered. *If only she knew about the man whom that street was named for.*

The big clock chimed once as Victor walked through the hotel lobby. Walton was on the phone again, as another couple stood in front of his desk. He looked busy.

Victor pushed the big heavy door open and was out on Park Street again. He turned left and walked the few steps to the corner. He turned left and began his journey over to the Children's Home. *I wonder what I'll find.*

Three blocks to Watt Street, a left turn, and just one block more. Victor noticed how little he remembered to watch his thoughts. Usually he was lost in them, thinking about the past, or whisked away by the future. Several times during his visit with Minnie, he thought this thought-watching was rather simple and obvious. More and more now, however, he was seeing that it wasn't.

This was a lovely old residential street; so quiet and shady. Majestic white sycamores lined the street on both sides, their boughs meeting high overhead. Low, cotton-ball clouds peeked through an occasional opening in the leafy dome. It was its own peaceful environment under here.

Victor spotted what must be the roof of his destination well before he exited the dark-green tunnel. It was an inviting red gabled roof, the shade of a red rubber ball, fresh and clean looking, not like many of the dark, moist, weathered ones on the homes he was passing.

He parried a slinging tree branch and high-stepped over the same tree's root rising from the middle of the sidewalk and emerged from behind what must have been a ten-foot-high wall of dense shrubbery.

There atop a gently sloping mound of neatly cut lawn, probably a hundred yards back off the sidewalk, rested the Children's Home. A white storybook picket fence ran along the sidewalk and disappeared at the bottom of the Home's rolling property.

"There it is," Victor said under his breath, a broad smile forming.

The 6,500 square foot house was enormous, much larger than Victor envisioned. It was a simple house, but its size made it special. A white, wood-frame house, with lots of plain windows. Four red-brick chimneys rose high above the roof, one on each outside wall of the home.

It appeared much taller than two stories; its floor was high above the ground to accommodate a complete basement with high windows that could be seen at ground level all along the sides of the house. The front porch was necessarily very high, and also extremely deep. A simple, neat, low shrub ran the perimeter of the house.

Only a few large trees stood in front, none close to the home. A few more were in back. Two stout ropes tied to a graceful aging limb of one of the trees dropped down some twenty feet and held a weathered old two-by-eight less than two feet above the ground. It swayed slightly in the breeze. Victor wanted to go swing on it.

The narrow, crowned gate in the simple white picketed fence was covered by a pergola, nearly invisible beneath the cascading ivy it supported. Victor cautiously opened the sturdy gate and grimaced when it creaked as he slowly and carefully closed and latched it. *What am I doing, trying not to wake anyone?* A cobblestone walkway meandered up to the front steps. Victor watched his steps and noticed how the grass grew between the smooth, slightly rounded stones. He considered that this was the very same house and property described in the article from 1899 that was in his pocket. *The ceremony must have taken place right there in front of me now—on this huge old porch. Mr. Watt may have walked these same cobblestones.*

Victor climbed the three flights of wide wooden stairs and took four long strides across the deep porch to the front door. It was difficult to step softly on the bare, enameled boards. Reaching up and taking hold of the gleaming brass door knocker, Victor inhaled deeply, rapped twice, and waited. He caught himself rocking sideways from one foot to the other and stopped. Then he noticed his clenched hands and relaxed them.

"Watch, watch, watch." He could hear Minnie's voice in his head. She must be napping now.

A smiling middle-aged woman opened the door.

"Hello," she said, pleasantly.

Smiling back, Victor began his well-practiced speech. "Hello. My name's Victor Truman, and I've come to speak with the director of the Children's Home."

"That would be Mr. McCully. Is he expecting you?" she asked, as if she already knew he had no appointments scheduled at this particular time.

"No, no he's not expecting me," answered Victor. "I have a very brief question concerning the founder of this home, Mr. Clement Watt."

"Oh, yes, Mr. Watt," she said, as if she hadn't heard that name in a long time. "Please, come in. I'll tell Mr. McCully you're here."

Victor thanked her and stepped into a large entry hall.

"I'll just be a moment," she said and turned to leave the room through a doorway on the opposite side of the room.

Victor considered it was good that she didn't invite him to sit—that maybe Mr. McCully would see him immediately.

At the end of the entry room was a fireplace with comfortable-looking chairs, end tables, and reading lamps. It looked very homey. Two portraits hung on either side of the brick fireplace. Although they were of different men, they all had similar qualities about them: serious, but concerned. Victor concluded that they were kindly men. *These must be the Children's Home's Directors since 1899. I wonder if Mr. McCully's picture is up there?*

Turning to the wall directly opposite him, Victor breathed in deeply, and his eyes widened. There, centered on the wall between two small electric wall lamps with tiny fabric shades was a very large oil painting in a heavy ornate wood frame. It was Clement! He looked older than he did in Minnie's picture of him, but there was no doubt, that was Clement. Victor stepped closer to study the painting. A small brass plate with block etched letters attached to the bottom of the frame confirmed it: Clement Watt, Founder. 1852-1933. *Since he was eighty-one when he died*, Victor calculated, *he was in his sixties when Minnie began to know him.*

Victor heard the woman's footsteps. She returned through the doorway and said with a smile, "Mr. McCully will be happy to see you now."

Great. Victor tried not to seem too excited. "Thank you very much," he smiled back, half bowing.

"Please follow me."

He took one last glance at Clement and felt a chill run through him, and followed her through the doorway.

They walked down a quiet hallway and the woman stopped and turned at a door at the end.

"Here's Mr. McCully's office," she said.

"Thank you again," Victor said, slowly entering the doorway. As he stepped through, there on his left was Mr. McCully, walking around a rather small desk, right hand extended, a pleasant smile on his face. Victor stepped toward him and they shook hands.

"John McCully," he said with an energetic handshake and confident smile.

"Nice to meet you, Mr. McCully. I'm Victor Truman."

"Please, have a seat." Mr. McCully gestured to one of the two simple wooden chairs angled in front of his desk.

"Thank you, sir." Victor sat and wondered if this chair was dreaded by all the children who lived here. Victor felt like a student, in a way.

"Mrs. Dowell tells me you're inquiring about our founder, Mr. Watt." Mr. McCully sat back and clasped his hands across his wide stomach. He appeared to be looking forward to this conversation.

"Mr. McCully," Victor shifted in the hard wooden chair, "I'm looking for information, but I don't know what it is." Victor suddenly felt a little foolish when he heard these words aloud. He felt his face and head get warm and wondered if Mr. McCully could see his embarrassment. *Watch, watch, watch.* He remembered Minnie's directions again and relaxed as best he could.

"I never knew Mr. Watt, of course," Mr. McCully began, "but I understand he was quite a man—very unassuming, very powerful, and extremely wise. I'm the fourth director to oversee the Children's Home, and it's run and operated according to strict guidelines set down, I'm told, by Mr. Watt himself."

Victor was surprised—but grateful—that Mr. McCully was saying so much so quickly. But now it was his turn to speak.

"Mr. McCully," Victor paused momentarily. Yes, he'd just better level with Mr. McCully; he had nowhere else to turn: "I discovered Mr. Watt's headstone in the old cemetery out by the Grand Hotel." He studied Mr. McCully's expression carefully. There was no reaction. "A date—August 4, 1899—is hidden in it." He kept watching for a reaction. Still none. "Since that's not his date of birth nor the date of his death, I assumed it's significant somehow." No change in Mr. McCully's demeanor. "So I dug up," *an interesting choice of words*, Victor thought, "this newspaper article from that date." Victor produced the copy from the worn white bag that had become his briefcase.

Mr. McCully looked interested now and carefully took the copy Victor held out. *Watch, watch, watch*, Victor remembered as he sat and waited for Mr. McCully to read the article. He smiled twice as he read every word. Victor's mind was racing, but he caught it and watched. He raised and lowered his shoulders to relax them. Then he noticed his forehead; it was tight, and he relaxed it. *There's so much going on in and around me*, he thought, *and I don't even know it most of the time*. He thought of Minnie.

Mr. McCully handed the copy back to Victor. He was silent for a moment as if in thought. Victor anticipated something—something big. But he remembered himself again and relaxed.

Mr. McCully was still leaning back in his chair, looking up at the ceiling, with a slight smile on his lips. Then his chair creaked and groaned and he sort of free-fell forward into an upright, sitting position. His hands were now clasped on the desktop. He acted as if he wanted to speak, but he wasn't speaking. Victor leaned forward, his eyes open wide, as if to say, "Yes, yes! What is it?"

Finally he spoke.

"Mr. Truman, please come with me."

Mr. McCully stood, but didn't look at Victor. He still had a kind of blank look, as if in thought. He left his office, with Victor following. They ended up back out in the entry hall at the wall opposite the fireplace and four pictures. Without a word, Mr. McCully turned to Victor and gestured with his left hand to two small frames hanging on the wall.

Victor smiled and looked at Mr. McCully briefly, and then zeroed in on the two frames. One was possibly a photo, but one of those old-fashioned types that looked like it could have been an extremely detailed illustration. It was of a large two-story house, with four chimneys, and a very large porch.

"That's *this* house!" Victor realized.

"Yes, in 1899." Mr. McCully looked like he was still trying to figure something out.

"And this one is a copy of the article I showed you!" Victor pointed to the second frame and moved in just inches away to read from it.

"Is Mr. Wheeler's picture one of those?" Victor turned and pointed back to the fireplace.

"Yes. He's at the top left side. The other three were his successors, and I follow them.

"But that's all I know." Mr. McCully's voice trailed off. He seemed to be trying hard to recall something that would solve Victor's puzzle.

Victor read enough of the original article to be sure it didn't contain some fact that his copy didn't. Then he turned to Mr. McCully with an expression that asked, "What now?" He looked back at Victor with a look that said, "I don't know how to help you."

Victor turned to the portrait of Clement Watt on the adjoining wall. "I wonder if he left a secret here," he said, speaking more to the picture than to Mr. McCully.

"From what little I know about him, I'd say you're onto *something*." Mr. McCully sounded very supportive; Victor appreciated that.

"Well, thank you very much for your time and help, Mr. McCully." Victor shook his hand, thanked him, and walked to the front door.

"What will you do now?" Mr. McCully asked.

"I think I'll go to the First National Bank and see the trustee of..." All of a sudden it dawned on Victor that Mr. McCully must know who that would be since that's probably who signs his paycheck.

Mr. McCully caught the same thought and continued where Victor left off. "...That will be Mr. Farmer, Mr. Tom Farmer. He's now the bank president and handles the endowment personally. Tell him I said hello."

"Where is the bank?" Victor asked.

"It's right on Park Street, across from the courthouse."

With renewed enthusiasm, Victor smiled and shook Mr. McCully's hand again.

"Mr. Tom Farmer. Great. That's where I'll go next. Thank you again, Mr. McCully."

"Not at all. And if I can help in any way, please, just ask."

Mr. McCully stood in the doorway awhile as Victor walked across the broad porch, down the steps, and along the cobblestone pathway.

Just before reaching the front gate, Victor stopped and turned around to face the house again.

The well! Where is the well? He scanned back and forth across the property but didn't see the well. What could have happened to the well? It should be somewhere close to the porch, as described in the article. He'd read it so many times, how could he forget the well?

I'd better go see Mr. Farmer, just in case the bank closes at three, he reasoned. If he doesn't know about the well, I'll come back and ask Mr. McCully.

Victor briskly retraced his route over to the Children's Home and calculated that it must be about two-thirty. He was hungry again, but there was no time to eat now.

Watch, watch, watch. Minnie's words came to mind again.

It was warm and humid. Victor kept up the pace, however, and before too long found himself back on the corner of Park Street and Second Avenue, where the Park Hotel stood, just down and across the street from the courthouse. Along the way back here, Victor had considered that he must have walked in front of the First National Bank on his way to the library, but he couldn't remember it. He turned left onto Park Street, walked along the block of shops and offices to First Avenue, and now stood at First and Park. There it was: one building in from the corner and right across from the grand courthouse building.

The First National Bank was a very tall, one-story, brick building. Its windows and doors matched the building: they were tall and narrow, too. Victor opened one of the twin front doors and entered. It was quiet and cool inside. A small counter with two teller stations stood to the right. The rest of the room was scattered with half a dozen desks. About the same number of people were either sitting behind the desks or walking quietly about, looking very efficient.

About halfway back, in the middle of the floor, with four leather chairs in front of it, sat the biggest desk of them all. A small rectangular nameplate was perched on its front edge. It read T. Foster.

A man who looked too young to be the manager of a bank sat behind it and was talking on the phone, head down, writing furiously with his free hand. Victor wondered if he knew he was sitting at his desk, talking on the phone, and writing furiously. He concluded that T. Foster was really nowhere in this bank; he was lost in thought, a million miles from here.

What Minnie had explained to him seemed so simple, almost *too* simple, this morning; but now, in just a few short hours, Victor was beginning to sense the weight of what she had taught him. *Everyone in this bank is really asleep mentally,* he realized. *They're all on autopilot!*

Victor stepped close enough to T. Foster's desk to let him know he was waiting to see him, but stayed far enough back to not be intrusive. As if by habit, Victor caught himself letting his eyes wander, not really seeing anything at all. He was asleep, too, along with the rest of these people!

He remembered himself and realized that he was nervous and self-conscious standing in the middle of the floor like this. *Watch, watch, watch.* He relaxed his knees and shoulders, and felt his face growing warmer and warmer as he saw how very nervous and self-conscious he felt. He caught himself biting his lip and relaxed his jaw and facial muscles. Then he noticed that his right foot was turned over on its side. This watching and relaxing was hard work.

Just when he noticed his hands tightly clenching the white bag they held in front of him, T. Foster spoke in Victor's direction.

"May I help you?"

Victor stepped up to the desk. "Yes, Mr. Foster, my name is Victor Truman. I'm here from Los Angeles to see Mr. Farmer." Victor thought calling him Mister, even though he couldn't be that much older than himself, was a good move to take, but the Los Angeles part may have been a bit too much. Maybe even misleading. Victor began to immediately worry, but he caught his face and forehead wrinkling with worry and relaxed them.

"Yes, Mr. Truman. Is Mr. Farmer expecting you?"

This could be trickier than it was with Mr. McCully. Better use the one ace he held.

"No, no he's not. Mr. McCully sent me over here." There, that should do it. Mr. Watt's Children's Home endowment must be one of the largest accounts in this bank. Victor noticed just then how he flipped from worried to nearly boastful in an instant.

"One moment, Mr. Truman. Won't you be seated?"

"Thank you."

Victor took the chair directly in front of him while T. Foster walked to a heavy oversized—probably mahogany—door to an office in the rear corner of the bank. There was a brass plate on it but Victor couldn't read it from here. T.

Foster knocked twice softly and then walked into the office, closing the door behind him.

Moments later he returned and said, "Mr. Farmer will see you now."

Victor thanked him and walked toward the big door. Mr. Farmer was standing as Victor entered. He wasn't smiling, but he seemed pleasant and calm. Just a busy man with lots on his mind. Victor guessed he was in his sixties. They shook hands and Mr. Farmer invited Victor to sit.

Mr. Farmer broke the ice. "So you know John McCully?"

"Yes, sir. Mr. McCully helped me with some research I'm doing on Mr. Clement Watt, the founder of the Children's Home." Victor then paused for a reaction or comment from Mr. Farmer. There was none. He continued: "I'm here on a trip from Los Angeles, and I discovered Mr. Watt's headstone in the old cemetery by the Grand Hotel." Still no reaction. "There's a date—August 4, 1899—hidden in the decoration. And since it's not his date of birth or date of death, I assume it must be significant in some way."

Mr. Farmer leaned back in his leather swivel chair, finger-tips touching and pressed against his lips. *Good. At least he looks interested.* But still, no comment was forthcoming.

"I searched the newspaper files, and on that very day was this article." Victor produced and unfolded the copy and handed it to Mr. Farmer. He paused and waited as Mr. Farmer read it. He acted as if he had never seen it, or if he did, it was bringing back pleasant memories. Victor remembered to watch himself. He saw that he was still nervous, but relieved, that Mr. Farmer didn't feel that Victor was wasting his time.

Mr. Farmer finished the article, handed it back, smiling. "My uncle was the very first trustee of the Watt endowment," he volunteered. *Good, he was beginning to warm up.* Victor waited for more, but there wasn't any.

"So I began researching the clues in this article to see why Mr. Watt considered August 4, 1899, important enough to hide in his headstone."

Mr. Farmer was thinking, and Victor waited. He noticed his hand was clutching the arm of the chair and relaxed it. He also noticed a thought going by that told him this was all just a big waste of time—his and everyone else's. Then he felt his forehead tighten in reaction to that thought. He relaxed again.

"It could be, Mr. Truman, that Mr. Watt was just so proud of the Children's Home...." Mr. Farmer's eyes traveled the office wall up to the ceiling. He was still thinking. Victor waited and watched.

"My uncle was very fond of Clement Watt." Mr. Farmer was speaking to the window as if Victor weren't there. Victor sat up straighter and anticipated some good information. "He didn't speak of him much, of course, their's being a fiduciary relationship and all, but I always knew my uncle respected Mr. Watt. That was unusual, for my uncle respected very few people." Mr. Farmer smiled, still looking out the window.

Victor smiled, too, and thought of Minnie.

"I knew Mr. Watt was a special man by the way my uncle spoke of him, as little as that was, and not just because of his vast wealth and position. Indeed, very few people actually knew the extent of his holdings and enterprises." Victor was all ears and wondered if Mr. Farmer had just stepped over the bounds of discretion. He hoped he'd keep going!

Mr. Farmer turned his chair around backwards and pulled a well-worn, leather-bound notebook about the size of a small-town telephone directory from a row of books and files standing along the top of the credenza behind his desk. He turned back and placed it on his desk in front of him. He touched its edges and looked down at it fondly, almost reverently.

"This is the directive laid down by Clement Watt to administer his children's trust. It is the clearest piece of writing I have ever seen in all my dealings in the financial industry, and that's been considerable." Mr. Farmer was smiling again, still looking down respectfully at the book. "Of course it contains the routine legal jargon, but when it comes to the home's day-to-day operation and the children's treatment, care, and education, you know this is an inspired document."

Show it to me! Victor's thoughts were shouting.

"I'm afraid I'm not at liberty to divulge any of its information, but I will tell you that whatever you can learn about Mr. Clement Watt will be a treasure to you your entire life. Again, I'm afraid that's all I can tell you."

Darn! Now what?

"I will tell you that I can recall no connection between that article and that specific date and these endowment instructions. I wish I could be of help."

"You have been, Mr. Farmer. Now, more than ever, I'm sure I'm onto something and should keep going." Victor stood and shrugged his shoulders. "But I just don't know where."

They shook hands again and Mr. Farmer spoke like a father to Victor. "Follow through, son, for you have everything to gain."

"Now what?" he muttered. Victor suddenly realized that he was experiencing a feeling that was very familiar to him: He was exuberant and ready, with nowhere to go!

Victor was standing out front of the First National Bank, staring out across the street at the huge courthouse building. His shoulders slumped as he realized he didn't even remember leaving Mr. Farmer's office, exiting the bank, and ending up here on the sidewalk. All that could have taken place an hour ago, or a day ago, for that matter. "Stay awake, Victor," he heard Minnie saying. As he remembered himself and came into the present, the words *Take the first step—no more, no less—and the next will be revealed* crossed his mind.

Those words had gotten him to where he presently was. And quite a monumental stride this had been! Four short days ago, if someone had told him all that was about to happen, he wouldn't have believed it. As he stood there in front of the bank, contemplating how C. W.'s prophetic message had already proved true, he realized that something was trying to push him along. What was telling him to rush and just *do something* at this moment? He stood firm and attempted to just watch the best he could. Although he couldn't identify any one thought in particular, the general message up there in his head was, *Get going! Don't just stand around!*

Victor stayed put. As agitated as his mass of thoughts became, he reasoned: *I've taken the first step and it led me here. Now I don't know what to do next. If I stay true to C. W.'s instruction, to take the first step—no more, no less—then the next will be revealed. The others just happened to come more quickly, apparently; this one's taking a little longer. So, I'll just wait and watch.*

He felt funny—nervous, actually—just standing there on the sidewalk. The thoughts were really hopping now: *You look stupid standing out here like this. People are watching you. You could get arrested for loitering. Someone inside the bank is going to*

come out and tell you to leave, or worse yet, call the police on you.
It was a never-ending barrage.

Never before had he examined what was going on in his
own mind like this. All that he learned this morning with
Minnie was making more and more sense. *These thoughts are
not in my best interest—obviously not! Why didn't I ever see that
before? It all seems so obvious, but so esoteric as well. The
thoughts parading through my mind right now are not for me—they
are against me! All right, that's the first step. And when I see that,
the next step is immediately apparent: Don't go along with those
thoughts. Don't do what they say!*

So Victor stood right there, refusing to give in and dash
off somewhere—anywhere!—just to appease these relentless
thoughts.

Two men were approaching from the direction of the
library on the corner. Victor was determined to stay put even
though the thoughts droned on and now had new ammuni-
tion: *Those two men are looking at you. They look like respectable
businessmen and won't think well of you. They both have families,
homes, two nice cars, kids in private schools, lots of money in the
bank.* Victor watched and just stayed put.

They were very close now and Victor could hear them
talking. Actually, they were doing more than talking; they
seemed to be almost arguing. One was saying, "Look! If that's
what he wants to do with the property, then I sure won't sell
to him. And no one can make me! I don't like it, and I won't
go along."

The other man then responded with an idea that must
have just struck him: "I've got it! That's it! There's no law
that says we can't put some C, C, and Rs in the deed...."

The first man was puzzled. "What are C, C, and Rs?"

"Covenants, Conditions, and Restrictions!" The second man boasted.

The two men walked right past Victor, not even aware that he was standing there. They weren't even aware that *they* were walking down this sidewalk, Victor realized.

Victor had heard Christine speak of C, C, and Rs before in connection with her various listings of homes in exclusive neighborhoods. There's a homeowner's association that comes up with a list of dos and don'ts that is actually a condition of living in that neighborhood. Things like you can only paint your home if the color you intend is approved by the association's architectural committee, you can't work on your car in view of the street, and you can't park a boat at the front curb.

Wait a minute! There must have been C, C, and Rs in Clement Watt's day, too! And a real property deed is about as permanent a document as there is! And, deeds are public records. Yes, the deed to the Children's Home. If Clement Watt could control anything from his grave, it would be the perpetually endowed Children's Home. Mr. Farmer just said how thorough and clear Mr. Watt was in his directions. And even though the directive may not be public, the deed *to the Children's Home surely is. The deed. That has to be it!*

Then the thoughts started again: *Yes, but what if you hadn't found the newspaper article—how would you have even known about the Children's Home?* Victor caught this doubt, and the wrinkles in his face that came with it. He relaxed. *It didn't matter what if, did it? The fact is, he had found the article!*

Victor took a deep breath. He smelled the natural fragrance of the air and felt its warmth and humidity on his face and arms. He relaxed his shoulders and hands. Back in the present, he looked up and there, right in front of him, stood the courthouse.

Victor crossed Park Street and Capitol Parkway, the circular street that separated the courthouse and made it an island in the park. He hurried up the broad walkway lined on each side by rosebushes, and high-stepped up the wide, curved stairs two at a time to one of the four enormous front doors under the columned portico. Judging by his own height, these doors must be over twelve feet tall.

He entered into a large anteroom with two doors in each of the three inside walls. A brass sign hung over each. The doorway to his immediate right was labeled Museum. That was very appealing, but the day was late and Victor needed to see that deed.

The door in the back corner to his left seemed to be the one: Land Records. The door opened into a small waiting area created by a stand-up countertop. Four wooden chairs stood against the wall facing the counter. Victor noticed that the countertop was solid—there was no section in it to enter or exit through. Various official-looking forms, announcements, and papers were neatly arranged in little stacks.

A woman in her forties, working diligently at her desk, heard Victor enter, but continued until she reached a good place to stop. She smiled pleasantly as she rose and stepped over to the counter.

"Hello," she said.

Victor smiled back. "Hello. Is this the office where I can get a copy of a property deed?"

"Yes it is."

"Good. I'm interested in the deed to the Children's Home on Watt Street—between Third and Fourth Avenues? I don't think it was named Watt Street at that time, though; I think it was Third Street then." Victor watched to see if she was following this. She was. If anything, she seemed to be way ahead of him. He continued: "Also, since a Mr. Clement Watt established the home as a foundation, the most recent deed will probably be one from him, or one of his companies, to the Children's Home Foundation itself.

"The Children's Home was dedicated in August of 1899, so I would guess that that deed would also be dated that year."

Her forehead furrowed. "Yes, I can search that deed by property address, but anything before about 1910 is archived now. And I'll only have a photocopy of the original deed. Those that old were mostly handwritten, so they're preserved and stored elsewhere. So I'll be searching our working copies and can produce a copy of that copy for you." She smiled as if what she just said was humorous.

"Well, that sounds good to me," Victor smiled back. "How long do you think it will take?"

"I'll submit this request to a clerk now, but since we're almost closed today, I would think I'll have it for you—well, likely before noon tomorrow."

"That'll be great," said Victor. "I'll see you then. Thanks very much."

Victor left the Land Records office and realized he had nothing to do until the deed was found. It was nearly four o'clock; he could visit the museum awhile, then catch the five o'clock van back to the Grand Hotel and return here on the one o'clock van tomorrow.

Victor walked diagonally across the foyer and slowly opened the big wooden door marked Museum. No one was in this rather small room with a very tall ceiling. The afternoon sunlight streamed in the tall palatine windows. Memorabilia covered the walls and filled several long, glass display cases.

This was more of a scrapbook room than a true museum, Victor thought, as he looked into the long glass case nearest the door. Mostly old letters, mementos, and newspaper accounts of the town's major events and leading citizens.

He moved to the next case and examined old photographs and a sample spike from the first railroad line through town. *Oh, and here's a photo of the dedication ceremony of the Civil War Cemetery where C. W.'s tombstone was later placed.* Victor studied this photograph carefully to see if he could recognize parts of it. *Yes, those cannons look familiar.*

He worked his way around the museum room and was standing at the case on the front wall, beneath the tall windows that looked so impressive from the street. The lawn, flower beds, and trees looked so peaceful outside. The hotel, shops, and businesses along the opposite side of Park Street were pretty as a picture. It was quiet here. The only noise came from Victor's footsteps on the shiny hardwood floor.

He took in a deep breath and closed his eyes. He felt the sun's warmth on his face and smelled the musty air in the room. He opened his eyes and looked down into the case before him. Waves of chills started at his head and ran down through his body to his feet. In the glass case, looking right at him, was a photograph of Clement Watt. A small hand-lettered card beneath it read: Clement Watt, founder of the Children's Home, August 4, 1899.

There was a calm, confident, peacefulness about him. There was such kindness and wisdom in his slight smile. Did he leave a secret message to be found? Minnie seemed to think so. Victor leaned forward on his toes, looking out the window behind the display case, trying to see Emma's board-ing house two blocks down Park Street. No, too many trees.

He looked back down into the glass case. Next to C. W.'s picture was a photograph of the Children's Home. *It's even warmer and homier-looking today. The trees are taller now. The lawn is thick and green. The hedges and vines are mature and full. There's the same white picket fence and little gateway, and the cob-blestone walk up to the large front porch. Perhaps C. W. did walk that same stone pathway. The well. Where's the well? It's nowhere in this picture.*

There, next to the two photographs was the newspaper article. Victor took his copy out and held it out to compare the two. Exactly the same. So C. W. *did* manage to preserve this article, this clue to his headstone's hidden message.

Victor was more confident than ever that he was on the right path, and that there *was*, indeed, a path. He had fol-lowed C. W.'s directions precisely: Take the first step—no more, no less—and the next will be revealed.

He was at that uncomfortable, but always rewarding, place again: the end of his thoughts, with no apparent next step in sight. And as he was learning, that's the right place to be, for the next step is always grander than anything his own mind can dream up. The secret is to simply remember this.

CHAPTER 9

Victor knew there was nothing else to do now but wait for the copy of the deed. There was still time to catch the five o'clock van back to the Grand Hotel, so he left the courthouse and enjoyed a brisk walk back through town. He walked past the picturesque shops and buildings along Main Street to the sturdy old oak tree standing in the cul-de-sac. The van was on time. Victor and an older couple were its only returning passengers.

He sat on the rear bench seat where he could stretch out and watch the passing countryside more comfortably. There were very few cars on the road. Victor thought of home, where at five o'clock in the afternoon the streets were jammed.

After miles of green, open spaces and bright blue skies, the van turned under the Grand Hotel entryway arch and on up the driveway to the welcoming porte cochere. As they pulled under and stopped, Victor realized he had not remembered himself even once since leaving town. This observation made him grimace, but the instruction came to him again: "Don't flinch, just watch." He smiled, and silently thanked Minnie.

Victor went straight to his room at the hotel. It felt good to be "home." It also felt good to be rid of this noisy paper bag that served as his attaché and suitcase all day. What a day it had been.

He freshened up, put on some aftershave, and went looking for Christine. As he walked through the hotel and around the grounds, he noticed how deeply absorbed others were in their thoughts; *they're walking on autopilot, miles away mentally.* He remembered himself again and vowed to stay awake the rest of the evening.

Five minutes later he was at the tennis courts and realized that he didn't remember walking there. A frown came over his face and even though he noticed it, another thought told him all this was useless, that to stay awake for any length of time is impossible. Then he remembered the blue rose.

Christine was playing singles with another agent. When she saw him, she dropped her racquet, ran out of the court, and hugged him.

"You look like Chris Evert out there," Victor smiled.

"Oh I missed you so much," she said, hugging him again. "Where did you get this snazzy shirt?"

"This? It's my tourist shirt; I blend in with the crowds. Now all I need is a video camera." *You can't even afford a video camera,* his thoughts reminded him. Victor caught that thought, relaxed away the tension that came with it, and silently addressed it: *Well, if you're so smart and all-knowing, show me how to afford one!* Doing this, he realized that all was well. All he had to do was stay out of those thoughts.

"Do you mind if we stop now?" Christine asked her friend.

"No, that's fine," the woman replied, "see you two at dinner."

Christine gathered her things, and she and Victor went back to their room to dress for dinner.

Although what Victor had just experienced amounted to the two most important days in his life—a true turning point—it wasn't something to be shared with others casually. And although Christine sensed the impact of his discovery from what little Victor had told her on the phone and this evening while dressing for dinner, they both contained the urge to speak of it among others.

Dinner dragged on and on. And what a different view of it Victor was now able to see. People talking incessantly, but not really even listening to each other. Victor noticed himself rushing through the meal. *Why?* he thought. *What's telling me to rush? Why can't I sit here calmly and enjoy this meal?*

Victor tried to see exactly what his thoughts were telling him that made him want to hurry. All he saw, however, were their effects: He was rushing. It occurred to him to deliberately slow down and see what would happen. The pressure increased. He still couldn't identify any particular thought, but he was watching the pressure build. It grew even more, and Victor finally just put his fork down, took a deep breath, and relaxed back in his chair. He did notice a thought that told him everyone else at the long table was watching him. Upon inspection, however, he saw that this was clearly not true. Everyone else was self-absorbed, lost in their own thoughts, and had no awareness that they were even here in this room having dinner.

Christine noticed what Victor was doing and asked him about it.

"If I don't know why I'm acting the way I am at any given moment, then I'm just a machine, and machines have no choices. What happens to them is just accidental. I noticed that I was rushing through dinner, a million miles away in thought, so I slowed down to see what it was my thoughts were saying that made me rush along."

Christine didn't understand completely, but she tried. Victor continued, half-whispering to his eager student.

"If I don't know that I'm sitting here in this room having dinner—as no one here does—then I'm lost in thought." Christine opened her eyes wider as if to say, Yes, go on.

"If I'm lost in thought, then I'm either mulling over something from the past, which is usually something painful, or I'm projecting something out into the future, which also is usually painful. So I'm usually living in a made-up dream and actually hurting myself. The only way to really live is to be right here—in the here and now—knowing what's *really* going on."

Christine was listening intently. "You mean like driving a car for miles and miles and not remembering anything about it?" she asked.

Victor considered her example for a moment and said, "Yes, I think so. The instinctual part of the brain obviously kept the car on the road and out of the lane of oncoming cars. But you—the driver—were lost in thought, somewhere in the past or future. And that can't be living, because the past and future don't even exist—they're just based on stored memories and projected fantasies."

Christine nodded and tried to sort out these new ideas.

Dinner was over and people began to leave the dining room. One of Christine's friends came over and suggested that they join her and her husband in the hotel theater where the movie *War Games* was being shown.

Christine looked at Victor. He could see that she wanted to go.

"Sure, let's go." Victor said. "I hope they have popcorn."

The showing began at eight o'clock, so they agreed to meet at the hotel's private theater a little before then.

The theater was down a hallway off the balcony that circled the hotel lobby's massive fireplace. It was a spacious room, but the low ceiling, windowless walls, and subdued lighting made it feel intimate.

Six rows of dark-brown leather chairs sat in the cool, dark, quiet room awaiting their audience. They were alternately spaced, so each had a clear view of the curtained wall at the front of the room.

Victor and Christine arrived before their friends and took chairs on the right side of the theater, halfway back. They sat and spoke in whispers about Victor's discovery as people began filtering in.

"Over here," Christine said in a hushed voice when she saw her friend and her husband. In this room, it just felt obligatory to whisper.

The four spoke of their secret vacation spot, what their activities had been, and someone asked about this movie, *War Games*. Christine's friend had heard conflicting opinions, some for and others against.

Just then the curtain covering the front wall slowly opened electrically to reveal a textured white screen. Within seconds the movie began.

From almost the opening scene, Victor grew more and more enthralled. "This is a movie all about thoughts," he excitedly whispered in Christine's ear. She shook her head to indicate that she didn't understand what he meant.

"I'll tell you later," he said.

War Games was a new angle on the best-seller *Fail-Safe*, which had been made into a movie in 1964 starring Henry Fonda and Walter Matthau. It was about World War III being triggered accidentally.

In *War Games*, David, a bright high school student who spends a lot of time at home on his computer, can even tap into his school's main computer and change grades.

Desiring to learn more about a new computer game on the market, he programmed his computer to automatically dial phone numbers in the vicinity of the company that produced this new game. His computer makes contact with another computer, but it's not the one he hoped to reach; it belongs to the U. S. Defense Department. This computer's purpose is to prevent World War III by making judgments based on its analysis of early warning systems and nuclear deterrents.

David challenges it to a game called "Global Thermo-nuclear Warfare" and the computer is delighted to oblige.

Since this "thinking" computer runs the United States' entire defense system, its activities are projected onto several huge screens in the underground war room command center. The small hotel audience was enthralled as *War Games* reached its climactic ending. But Victor was the most wide-eyed and compelled of all. Because of what Minnie explained, he realized that he was watching a very accurate demonstration of the human brain in operation. Knowing this, one could plainly see the mental error people make that prevents them from attaining the life they truly desire.

As David's and the computer's nuclear "war" between the United States and Russia unfolded on the screens before them, the U.S. General and his staff were baffled, and panicked. They were watching the elements of a full-scale nuclear war come together, but couldn't verify—or deny—its authenticity.

The computer was in control. David asked it if this was a game they were playing or the real thing.

"What does it matter?" the computer replied.

With only a few hours remaining before the computer began launching nuclear warheads toward Russia, David finally located the computer's programmer and brought him to the command center.

He can't stop the computer, but explains that, although it can learn, it never learned futility; that is, it doesn't know the value of giving up. So their only hope is to attempt to engage it in a "thinking" process whereby it can learn futility.

They begin suggesting games that would demonstrate this to the computer. The programmer asked his group of assistants if any of them still play Tic-Tac-Toe. They all said no.

"Why?" he continued. "Because you see the futility in it. Once you know the secret of Tic-Tac-Toe, it's futile to play because no one ever wins—it always ends in a tie."

So they challenged the computer to a game of Tic-Tac-Toe. When the computer asked how many players, they answered "Zero" which meant the computer would play against itself.

While the nuclear war escalates, and some 2,400 Russian missiles were launched and headed for their U.S. targets on the screens before them, the general wants to retaliate and immediately launch our missiles in a counter-attack.

But the programmer understands the computer and tries to convince the general that what he sees on the screens before him is just a machine's hallucination. "It's a bluff. Don't respond like a machine," the programmer tells him.

As the general fights his impulse and training to react and respond, the computer begins playing game after game of Tic-Tac-Toe, until it's racing through every possible combination of moves at lightning speed.

The tension builds as Russia's missiles are just seconds away from striking their targets, when the Tic-Tac-Toe games cease and another series of calculations fills the primary screen: The computer is applying what it just learned from playing—and finally understanding—Tic-Tac-Toe to every possible combination of nuclear confrontations.

When the computer concludes that neither side would win in scenario after scenario streaming by at nearly the speed of light, the big screen suddenly goes blank. The room is silent, the screens are dark, the computer is thinking.

The big screen twinkles as the computer announces its conclusion: A strange game. The only winning move is not to play.

Victor was electrified. This was a movie about how we think! It's so obvious, but we can't see the only logical, obvious solution. We can't see the forest for the trees.

Obviously. Victor heard two couples leaving the theater discussing the movie's "flaws." He understood Minnie's comment about being wiser than the world a little better.

Christine and her friend were partners in a tennis tournament, and had to be ready early the next morning, so they decided against having a late treat and coffee. They said their good nights and left the theater for their rooms.

Victor explained—two or three times—how what Minnie had revealed to him about our thoughts, and our misunderstanding of them, was so dramatically and clearly shown in *War Games*. Christine tried to follow his excited explanations, but Victor saw that she was tired and needed to sleep.

He had trouble falling asleep, reflecting on this important day's "coincidental" events. He anticipated what might lay in store for him tomorrow. That's when he remembered to watch, instead of be, his thoughts. His forehead was furrowed, his hands were clenched, his legs were twisted under the covers in the strangest fashion.

Victor repositioned himself in a natural, comfortable position, and kept watching. Then he noticed how rapid and shallow his breathing was; he consciously slowed and deepened it.

It occurred to him that his mind *wanted* to project how tomorrow was going to unfold. He noticed how it just raced along, thousands of thoughts speeding by, that very few could even be singled out and examined. His mind, he saw, was relentless. No wonder Minnie called it a "beast." (computer)

As he caught his thoughts again projecting tomorrow's events, he thought of the movie they had just seen. It dawned on him that his mind could not possibly know, or project, what would happen tomorrow—how could it? *But then, isn't this what worry and anxiety are all about? Aren't worry and anxiety simply ignorant projections that can't possibly be based in reality?* Minnie's words came to him: "There is something enormously wrong with how we think."

Can this really be true? Could this whole world be suffering the consequences of one grand delusion? What a prospect.

CHAPTER 10

Victor awoke with the sunrise. The morning light was dim in the window. A blue jay squawked in bursts outside. Christine still slept, and Victor used this time to quietly watch his thoughts.

Lying still, aware of his breathing and moving chest, he noticed his eyes darting about the room, unwilling to settle on one object. *What told them to be so restless? Some thought must be giving them orders, but I can't see it or sense it. And something doesn't want me to lie here in bed like this. But what is it?*

After several minutes of this, he noticed his face and forehead tighten with an expression of frustration. He couldn't catch a thought, but then realized one just told him he failed miserably at this thought-watching business. That's when he caught the tightness in his face and forehead. He remembered Minnie's instructions to not react, just watch. He relaxed and began again.

No wonder nothing new enters my mind, Victor considered. *I'm so busy at the beck and call of these thoughts that I don't even see, there's no room for anything new; I'm never present enough to see it anyway!* He knew he had just received a valuable clue to the importance of staying present, and the value of separating himself from these invisible, never-ending task masters.

Victor realized he was lost in thought again when Christine had awakened and actually gotten out of bed before he knew it. Another shock and pang of disgust shot through his mind. *Just watch, don't react. But what a waste of time,* a thought told him. *Maybe,* he considered, *but if I don't attempt to stay present and out of this rush of negative, destructive thoughts, I'll just be lost in it. If I don't try, then I'm already defeated.* He noticed his breathing again, something he hadn't done since twenty minutes ago when he began this exercise.

"Good morning! You ready for the big tournament?"

"I think so," Christine said, stretching and yawning. "Want to have breakfast together?"

"Sure. That'd be nice. The deed is supposed to be ready by noon, but I thought I'd take the nine o'clock van into town just in case they find it sooner."

"Good. If we hurry, maybe we can get a nice walk in around the grounds after breakfast. I'm due at the courts at nine also."

They dressed and were in the dining room at a table next to the picture-window wall well within an hour. Christine ordered a fruit plate and Victor was enjoying eggs, bacon, and grits.

"There really is something to all this you stumbled onto, isn't there." Christine spoke as if they had been discussing the topic all along, which they hadn't. The answer was obvious, but Victor reiterated what they both already knew.

"Absolutely. This is what I've—we've—been searching for, and it was right here, under our noses, all the time. It's the only thing that makes perfect sense. But it's not easy. Have you noticed how little you know where you are and that you're even breathing? Isn't it shocking to realize how deeply asleep we are?"

"Yes, I've begun to notice that."

"Everyone else in this room—in the whole world!—thinks they're alive and well, but all you have to do is just look at them—at us—to see how deeply asleep and frightened they are."

"I was thinking about being on the tennis court yesterday and how poisonous my thoughts are. They were telling me that I looked fat and ugly out there running around, that people were laughing at me, that I'd never be good at tennis, that I wasn't a good mother and wife, and on and on; it was relentless. It's a wonder we make it through life as well as we do, carrying this tremendous burden.

"Then I thought how impressionable small children, especially, are, and how they can be severely damaged because a cruel parent will tell them over and over that they're no good, that they are bad, that they'll never amount to anything. Well, the child usually believes all these lies because they come from a source the child believes without question—its parent or elder. And then it occurred to me just last night that we—adults—listen to and believe these thoughts in our head without question. But if we'll just stop a moment and take a look at them—how horrendous!"

Victor smiled proudly at Christine. She knew. She understood the treasure Victor had found here.

"Let's go for that walk," he said.

They had walked for nearly an hour, meandering the paths and clearings around the hotel. It was a hot, tropical morning, but the lush setting and fragrant scents made one forgive the humidity.

Christine and Victor were coming up a knoll to the tennis courts, still discussing their discovery.

"If I hadn't run into Minnie or whatever else I may find here yet, we would still be like that computer in the movie last night: all set and prepared to wage war, believing that that's the only way. But like the programmer who sent the computer in a totally new direction so it could learn for itself the futility and destructiveness of its present path of understanding, Minnie—or C. W.—has shown us another direction that leads to a completely new outcome.

"I just noticed how little I've been here mentally on our walk this morning."

"Me too," Christine whispered.

"So I think the point is, like Minnie taught me, just to see it. Obviously, I can't change it; all I can do is just see it. Seeing how lost I am is certainly better than being lost and not knowing it.

"Here we are. Go get 'em, champ! And no matter what those thoughts tell you, I say you're the prettiest, most graceful of all!"

Christine hugged and kissed him good-bye and Victor left the tennis courts to catch the van into town.

He sat in the back of the van again. Six others came aboard and soon they were underway. Victor resolved to stay awake the entire trip into town, but they had barely cleared the hotel's entry arch when he realized he had not even been aware of his own breathing. Darn! And then he remembered: *Don't react, just observe. Be an impartial observer.* He started over.

The smooth ride and cool air inside the van made it very easy—even tempting—to drift into mental sleep. He maintained a determined effort, however, and managed to be present in the here and now for several short stretches.

The old covered bridge was just ahead. Victor readied himself to get a good look at the *Coincidental* when they crossed over the bridge.

The driver slowed the van and with a slight bump they were on the wooden planks of the bridge. Victor looked down the river. The boat was gone; the *Coincidental* wasn't there. He turned and looked up river but saw only two small fishing boats drifting along.

As the van pulled into the cul-de-sac and came to a stop, Victor caught his mind racing. It began the moment he discovered the *Coincidental* missing. Faster than he could see, his mind drew conclusions, changed those conclusions, and made assumptions. In those few brief moments, those thoughts took Victor through a whirlwind of emotions—from elated to depressed, from hopeful to forlorn. All this turmoil because the *Coincidental* wasn't there. And all this based on no evidence at all. His mind had no knowledge whatsoever, except that the *Coincidental* wasn't docked where it was two days ago, yet it reeled off a multitude of imaginings that sent his emotional system gyrating.

Victor considered how much energy he must have expended in just the past few seconds—not even one minute!—and how it would have served him much more profitably to have remained in the present.

Thanking the driver as he left the van, Victor headed down Main Street into town. The clock post showed nine-forty-seven as he turned left onto First Avenue. He noticed himself rushing and made a deliberate effort to slow his pace. It was as if a stiff tail wind was pushing him along. But it wasn't anything so obvious as that—it was just those invisible thoughts.

He crossed Watt Street, where the automobile traffic began, and looked down it to see if the Children's Home was visible. No, those towering old trees providing a tunnel over the street blocked the view. Coming up on First Street now, he tried to look through the glare in the front windows of the Daily Gazette building and see Mr. or Mrs. Jessup.

There was the courthouse, a block away but still imposing in its size and stature. Since he had been in it, and now that he had business there, it was familiar rather than intimidating. Thoughts still streamed through Victor's mind, telling him how foolish this search of his was. They told him there was no secret, nothing to be found, and that he was impractical and irresponsible to be expending all this time and energy on nothing but a childish wild-goose chase.

When Victor caught these thoughts, he stopped abruptly in his tracks on the sidewalk. Then a whole new barrage of thoughts came: *What are you doing? People are staring at you! Get going, you have to get to the courthouse! That deed's probably ready! Move!*

He stayed put and saw more clearly than he ever had just what was going on here. First the thoughts told him that this was all just an irresponsible, childish waste of time. Then when he actually, physically, stopped his pursuit—as those thoughts told him to do—they rallied again, shouting to not stop, but to keep pressing on! Very strange.

Amid the flurry of rushing, conflicting thoughts coursing through his mind, Victor more fully realized what Minnie had taught him and what Clement's note to her in the Bible meant: *Always seek "the impossible." Its solution lies just beyond your mind.*

This had to be what that instruction meant. *Now that I've seen how my mind is filled with nothing but chaos and conflict, how can I trust it? So how can I mentally stand aside and watch this all taking place? That's the great lesson Minnie taught me, or I might never have known there was a life outside all this turmoil. And this is what Clement was trying to teach Minnie.*

Come to think of it, this is also what he meant in his speech: For things are not what they seem. In the world's broad field of battle, in the bivouac of Life, be not like dumb, driven cattle! Be a hero in the strife! Trust no future, howe'er pleasant, let the dead past bury its dead. Act, act in the living present. Heart within, and God o'erhead.

"Just beyond your mind" means "no future" and "the dead past." Stopping and taking a good look at what's going on in my mind is "just beyond" it. So this is where my Heart is, with "God o'erhead."

A sense of calm swept through him; a feeling of tranquility.

Victor looked over at the courthouse and crossed Park Street, deliberately walking more slowly than those thoughts told him to. It occurred to him that the way it mostly was now, he was a slave to the thoughts in his mind, and that his task was to reverse this: His job was to actually change the way his mind now operated so that these thoughts became the slave and not the master. He also considered that, based upon what he learned from Minnie, this transformation could not be brought about by force or will, but just the observation of the entire process would bring about the change.

All this, in less time than it took him to cross over to the other side of Park Street. Now his mind was telling him to go eat first and then check in at the Records office. *But I did just eat*, Victor silently responded. He actually looked back over his shoulder at the dining room windows in the Park Hotel when he realized that his thoughts had control of him again. *This is impossible*, he thought. *These thoughts are too overpowering.* Then he recalled C. W.'s note to Minnie in the Bible and remembered himself again.

Victor bounded up the steps to the courthouse and pushed open one of its tall, heavy doors. His footsteps made sharp, hollow sounds across the floor. He entered the Land Records office and saw four people gathered around one of the desks, all looking down intently at some paperwork. One of the two men looked up and spoke to Victor.

"Yes, may I help you?"

"Ah, yes," said Victor, nervously. Just then he noticed his nervousness and tried to see its cause. "I was in yesterday and spoke to a woman here about obtaining a copy of an old deed—from 1899." Victor quickly studied the two women around the desk. Yes, the one who helped him was there. She looked up and smiled.

"Oh, yes. Hello there. Yes, your deed was brought in very soon after we opened this morning. Apparently they had no trouble locating it among the old records."

"That's great," said Victor. He noticed his hands were clenched and relaxed them.

"Let's see, your envelope is right over here." She went to another desk and picked up a very wide, very long brown envelope with a waxed-string and fastener attached. She unwound the string, opened the envelope flap, and pulled out a single sheet of white paper. Walking to the counter where Victor stood, she began looking it over.

"Yes, this is the most recent deed recorded on the property, if you could call it recent—it was recorded," she turned the paper sideways, "in May of 1899." She smiled and handed it to Victor.

He was very excited and noticed his hands shaking as he took the copy. He could see it had all been originally handwritten. He was handling it very gingerly and then realized this wasn't the original and wasn't delicate. The woman noticed this and smiled.

"Oh, this is wonderful, just fantastic!" Victor said, his mind racing now. All he wanted to do was go sit someplace and study every inch of it. "How much is the fee for this?"

"Five dollars," the lady replied.

Victor laid the copy on the counter and pulled five dollars out of his wallet. *It's worth five hundred—even five thousand!* he thought to himself.

"Thank you *very* much for your help," Victor said, picking up his prize.

"Not at all," the lady replied. "I hope it's what you're looking for."

Victor smiled, turned for the door, and the next thing he knew, he was standing on the front steps outside the courthouse. *Where was I the last few moments? I don't even remember walking from the Records office, across the foyer, and out the front doors. Insidious. Yes, that's a very accurate term to describe how thoughts operate.*

It was a splendid day, even with the heat rising. The trees and flowers around the courthouse were all so fresh and vibrant. Victor inhaled a deep breath of clean park air and decided to sit down right here, on the edge of a large planter, and enjoy every word of this deed.

He chuckled to himself. Here he was, like a child on a trip to Disneyland, all worked up over a copy of an old deed.

It looked almost a hundred years old: completely handwritten, even the recording mark was dated and signed by hand. There was the title—Land Deed. Then a meets-and-bounds description of the property running for several paragraphs. *It's a wonder they got so much information all on one page; the handwriting isn't all that tiny. Maybe the original deed is larger and this copy was reduced to fit on one page by the photocopying machine.*

Here's some legal mumbo jumbo, but from what I can tell, Clement Watt deeded the property from his own name over to the Children's Home Foundation, with directions that it be governed according to its by-laws.

Here it is! "This grant is in fee simple and it is conditioned upon the foundation of preserving the statue of the well I have placed on the property. It must henceforth and forever remain on this property, completely visible and accessible both to the property's residents and visitors alike."

That's it! Victor read it again. *Now what's so special about that well?*

As Victor waited for someone to open the door, he wondered if he looked presentable. He practically ran to the Children's Home from the courthouse and was still out of breath. He straightened his hair and wiped his brow with his fingers.

Mrs. Dowell answered the door.

"Hello, Mrs. Dowell. If you recall, I'm Victor Truman. I was here yesterday meeting with Mr. McCully."

"Yes, Mr. Truman. Nice to see you again."

"I know I'm always showing up unannounced, but could I see Mr. McCully for just a few moments?"

"Oh, he's not here just now. He's hosting a group of gentlemen on a river cruise this morning. I expect him back after lunchtime."

"You mean the *Coincidental?*"

"Yes. Have you seen it?"

"Yes, I first saw it two days ago on the river. Then it was gone this morning as I came into town."

"They left rather early this morning," she smiled.

"Mrs. Dowell, in the newspaper account of the dedication ceremony of this home back in 1899, a statue of a well with an inscription on its roof was mentioned. Is that well still on the property?"

"Why, yes. It's just around back, down a little path to a slight clearing."

"Would it be okay if I went down to look at it?"

"Oh, yes, by all means. Certainly it's all right. Just go on down and take your time."

"Thank you, Mrs. Dowell. Thank you very much."

Victor wondered if Mr. McCully had said anything about himself or the reason for his visit yesterday. Anyway, she certainly was kind and cordial.

He left the big broad porch and walked on the lawn around the house to the back. Several children played in the yard while a young girl in her teens supervised. She looked up as Victor came around the corner. Not wanting to startle her, he pretended he was lost.

"Hello. I'm looking for the statue of the well. Mrs. Dowell said I'd find a path to it back here."

A little boy, playing with a frog on the lawn between Victor and the young girl, intervened: "Yes, sir. Follow the footpath over yonder down to that big ole oak tree," the lad said matter-of-factly, pointing to the top of a large oak tree that peeked over the backyard knoll.

"Well, thank you, young man." Victor bowed in appreciation to the small boy and looked over and smiled at the young girl. She returned his smile and giggled.

He spotted the path the boy pointed out at the top of the knoll. The oak tree came into full view at the bottom of the rise. Journeying down, winding and descending through a thicket, he came to a clearing. There in the center sat the well.

"Look!" Victor said aloud. Here was the very well—nearly a hundred years old—that he had read of in the *Daily Gazette* article. But it sure wasn't situated the way he imagined from reading the article.

I pictured it to be right next to the porch, which I now know was the back porch, where the ceremony took place.

It was a simple well, made of bronze, with an A-shaped roof. About three feet in diameter, it stood about six feet tall. Victor faced the side of the roof and read its inscription:

> For things are not what they seem.
> In the world's broad field of battle,

In the bivouac of Life,
Be not like dumb, driven cattle!
Be a hero in the strife!
Trust no Future, howe'er pleasant!
Let the dead Past bury its dead!
Act,—act in the living Present!
Heart within, and God o'erhead!
　　—from *A Psalm of Life*
　　by Henry Wadsworth Longfellow

"That's from a Longfellow poem! The newspaper article made them seem like C. W.'s own words. How come Minnie didn't say something? Maybe she thought I knew the poem," Victor was whispering aloud and suddenly realized it. He looked around to see if anyone was nearby. No, but he could hear the children playing not far off, up over the top of the knoll.

He had the same feeling that he experienced in the cemetery, only it was stronger now. C. W. had actually led him to this very spot! It was almost spooky to consider. He wondered if anyone else had been led here in the same way.

Victor read Longfellow's words on the well's roof again. *Is this C. W.'s secret? I understand more of what it means, but only because I met Minnie. Now is how, don't live in thought. But, like Minnie even said, C. W. couldn't have counted on anyone reading his headstone to meet Minnie so she could help explain it. What now?*

Take the first step—no more, no less—and the next will be revealed.

Victor stood still and remembered himself. He was aware of his breathing; he relaxed his face, shoulders, arms, hands, and

legs. The last time he remembered to do this was a few minutes
ago on the front porch, when he was talking to Mrs. Dowell.

"Darn!" he said sharply, clenching his hands into fists.
"Why can't I remember?" But then he recalled Minnie's words
again: "Watch, watch, watch. Don't react, just watch." He
relaxed again. *Take the first step—no more, no less—and the next
will be revealed. I wonder what's on the other side of the roof?*

He walked around the well and—writing! "All who seek
an answer here can find it."

*And a skeleton key under the quote. That's the same key that's
on C. W.'s headstone. Yes, exactly the same. And facing the same
direction. I looked at that key long enough in the cemetery to know
it anywhere.*

No name, no source. *All who seek an answer here can find
it. Well, that's me. I'm here now. What is it? Where is it?*

Victor stepped back, away from the well, to the edge of
the small clearing to assess the whole picture.

*Is this a meditation garden? No, if it were meant to be that,
the well would be over there, under that beautiful, graceful oak
tree. That's the perfect spot for this well, but C. W. didn't place it
there. No, this well is deliberately out-of-place; it's close enough to
the house to be accessible and not forgotten, but it's far enough
away to not be an attraction. It's far enough away to make someone have a purpose and a desire to visit it, but it's not inviting
enough to lure someone out here. There's no shade, no benches to
sit on, no flowers or gardens. But it's here, and C. W. wanted it to
always be here or he wouldn't have said so in the deed.*

Victor walked to the well again and touched its roof. The
metal was warm, very warm, from the sunlight coming from
almost directly overhead now. He bounced the heel of his
hand on the bronze roof. Sturdy. He looked down into the

well. At the bottom was just dirt, a few weeds, and some small stones. He leaned under the roof and whistled into the well. The tone resonated and was amplified under here. He whistled again, louder this time, and heard a slight echo. He did it once more.

Victor knelt beside the little well and looked up under the roof. It was flat. The roof had a flat base across the bottom. That meant it was hollow inside. He rapped his knuckles up against it. Yes, it's hollow. He knocked on the outside of the roof. Yes, it's definitely hollow.

He leaned in under the roof again and twisted around until he was looking directly up at its base. This was an uncomfortable position, like a mechanic under a car, or a limbo dancer maneuvering under the bar.

Even in broad daylight, it was dim under here; it took a few moments for Victor's eyes to adjust. At one end he saw a separation. This base sheet of bronze was actually two sheets fitted together—one large piece and this smaller section about eight inches wide. He ran his fingers across the smooth surface, feeling for hinges or bolt heads. *Nothing. But there! There in the corner of this smaller section is a hole!*

His neck muscles cramping, Victor leaned in closer. *It's not a round hole; it's oblong...like a skeleton key would fit. There's a key to this compartment—a skeleton key. Why else would it be on his headstone and on this well?* Victor felt around under the well's roof, every inch of it. He pressed his finger up against the keyhole and looked at the impression it made in the fleshy fingertip.

"Yep, look at that: A skeleton key fits this keyhole!" He spoke out loud and looked around again. He walked his fingers over every bit of the well from top to bottom. He leaned over inside the well, feeling the sides and dirt bottom for a key, another compartment, anything.

Victor surveyed the ground around the well. Could C. W. have buried the key to the compartment? No, that would be too iffy. In the deed, he just stipulated that this well remain *on* the property, not in this very spot. It could theoretically be moved.

All who seek an answer here can find it. Take the first step— no more, no less—and the next will be revealed. Victor remembered himself and relaxed. He watched the flock of thoughts that had descended upon him. Calmly seeing them from this new vantage point, he understood more clearly than ever that they didn't know what to do either. It surprised him to realize they were like an angry, confused mob.

He read Longfellow's words again on the roof of the well in front of him:

> For things are not what they seem.
> In the world's broad field of battle,
> In the bivouac of Life,
> Be not like dumb, driven cattle!
> Be a hero in the strife!

What else could Longfellow have been describing but the conflict and confusion—the war!—that was taking place in his mind this very moment?

> Trust no Future, howe'er pleasant!
> Let the dead Past bury its dead!
> Act,—act in the living Present!
> Heart within, and God o'erhead!

What else could this mean but to separate myself from this turmoil of thoughts and "act in the living Present"?

"Hello there!"

Victor turned to see who was calling. It was Mr. McCully! It didn't look like him at first—he was dressed casually in khakis and a sport shirt.

"Oh, hello, Mr. McCully." Victor's first thought was to not let him near the well, but then he realized that was a stupid thought. If McCully knew of the secret compartment, he wasn't telling, and if he didn't know about it, then it wouldn't matter.

McCully walked down the path to the well and Victor began walking up the path to meet him.

"I came back to see if the well Mr. Watt unveiled at the dedication ceremony was still here. Mrs. Dowell directed me to it."

"Oh, yes, yes. I should have mentioned it to you myself yesterday. It's a handsome well isn't it?"

"Yes, indeed." Victor concluded that McCully had no knowledge of the hidden compartment. But he also was the only one Victor knew to ask. "Mr. McCully, let me show you something I discovered."

Victor walked over to the well and McCully followed him around to the back side of the roof with C. W.'s quote, All who seek an answer here can find it. Victor stood and looked at it as McCully read it aloud.

"Clement Watt spoke these words at the dedication ceremony, did he not?" McCully asked.

"Yes, according to the newspaper account, he did." Victor answered, his arms folded across his chest as if evaluating a fine painting in a museum. "But what intrigues me, Mr.

McCully, is that key beneath the quotation. That key is the very same one on Mr. Watt's headstone in the cemetery."

McCully looked at Victor, but it wasn't a puzzled look, it was an expectant expression on his face.

Now Victor was not only puzzled about the key; this strange look on McCully's face was unexpected—something he had to resolve.

Victor took a deep breath and came back to the present, relaxing as best he could. He looked at McCully a few moments more and then asked the only question that would resolve this rather strange situation: "Mr. McCully, do you know something about this key?"

"Come with me." That's all McCully said, and then he started back up the foot path.

From the tone in which McCully had just spoken, Victor thought it best to say nothing more. He followed McCully in silence back to his office. It was silent because neither spoke a word on the way, but in Victor's mind, at least, there was anything but silence. His head was wild, on fire now with flaring thoughts. He observed how the less it actually knows, the more animated and agitated the mind becomes.

Victor mentally ordered his mind to quiet down, but he saw that this had the same result that fanning a flame or shouting at a lion would. Then he remembered Minnie's lessons and just did his best at watching the mental melee taking place within him.

Mrs. Dowell was in the hallway outside McCully's office as they came through.

"Mrs. Dowell, please hold any calls for me," he said as he opened his office door and waited for Victor to enter first. "Please have a seat."

"Thank you." Victor's voice was calm and quiet, but it belied his inner condition.

McCully walked to a bookcase on his wall and reached up to a shelf over his head. Standing on his toes, he felt around among some books and produced a small, polished, dark wooden box.

Cigars? Victor thought. *C. W. liked cigars. No, too small.* His heart was beating faster. McCully returned to his high-backed leather desk chair, placed the box on the leather blotter in front of him, opened the box, and lifted out an exact replica of the key—the key Clement Watt displayed on his headstone and the roof of the well!

Smiling, McCully solemnly half-stood at his chair, leaned over his desk, and handed it to Victor.

Victor's mouth hung open and his eyes were wide. Carefully accepting it with both hands, the key was heavier than its small size led one to believe.

The key! Victor stared at it, turning it side to side and end over end, memorizing every detail. It was a handsome key.

"Why didn't you tell me about this yesterday? I might have never come back here."

"You didn't ask." McCully's voice was sympathetic.

"But you knew I was onto something. I was searching...."

"When I officially took on this position, the very first day this office became mine, I was given instructions—explicit instructions—that should anyone, whomever he or she may be, ever inquire about this key, I was to turn it over to him or her without question. But only if they specifically asked for it."

"Do you know what it opens?" Victor expected him to say yes.

"I know very little about that key. I do not know what it opens. Indeed, you obviously know more than I do about it. And, per my instructions, it is yours now." He smiled again.

"Has anyone else ever asked for it?"

"Per my instructions, I cannot say."

Victor sensed from the way McCully replied that there had been others, but he knew any more questions about them would not—could not—be answered.

"Is there anything else I should ask you, Mr. McCully?" He couldn't resist asking this, hoping to cover all bases.

McCully smiled. "No, there's nothing more I can help you with."

Victor was grateful that McCully wasn't asking *him* questions—how he came to ask for the key and what he supposed it opened, in particular.

"Well, I guess this is it." Victor stood, holding the key tightly. He extended his hand. "Mr. McCully, thank you very much for your help and kindness."

"It was my pleasure. And I've certainly enjoyed meeting you, too."

They shook hands and Victor departed, anxious to test his theory.

CHAPTER 11

$\mathcal{V}$ictor descended the home's front steps, walked around behind the house, and made his way along the path to the well.

Once at the well, Victor looked around. No one was in view from this spot, and only someone looking out from one of the upper story windows would be able to see him from the house. He assumed those would be the children's sleeping quarters.

Victor held the key tightly, leaned in under the well's roof, and placed the tip of the key into the small opening he had discovered. Turning the key back and forth slightly, he pressed it upward. Something inside the opening gave way and the key slid into the keyhole almost a full inch. He was moving slowly and deliberately, but now his heart began to beat faster.

He turned the key counterclockwise but it barely moved. He turned it clockwise and it moved farther. With slightly more pressure and a little jiggling, the lock yielded. Click! He relaxed his grip on the key, and it just hung from the keyhole. Taking hold of it with both hands and carefully pulling the key, but simultaneously using his hands to support the metal door, Victor worked, applying and releasing pressure.

Then the resistance gave way. Victor relaxed his support and the hinged piece of metal slowly lowered. Small particles of dust scattered in the sunlight. Victor expected something to fall from this little attic he had just opened under the roof of the well. But the door hung there, open and silent.

Victor looked up into the attic to pure darkness. He carefully placed his hand up inside the opening and felt around the edges. It was smooth and dusty inside. He removed his hand to check for insects; his fingers were coated with a thick layer of fine dirt.

Reaching in again with one hand, he felt farther in, keeping his fingers off the metal floor of the attic. The air was very warm inside. As he reached in even deeper, toward the opposite end of the roof, he touched a wooden box. He carefully felt its corners, patted its top, and pushed it slightly to ascertain its weight. It was about the size of a cigar box, and very light.

Having no idea what it might be, Victor cautiously slid the thin box toward the opening. Using his other hand, he lowered it into view. Something was inside, but it was very lightweight. He carefully set the dusty old box down on the edge of the well. Victor inhaled deeply and noticed that just about every part of him was tense with anxiety. He exhaled slowly and watched much of this tension leave.

Still not knowing what to expect, he inspected the box visually on all sides. Then he tilted it up on one edge and looked at the bottom. Nothing that unusual: just a simple wooden box, about seven inches by ten inches by two inches, with two small dark-metal hinges on the long side. A small metal hook clasped around a tiny nail held the lid closed.

He carefully picked the box up and gently shook it. There was something soft inside; it made a sliding sound. He set the box down again and slowly pushed the clasp off of the nail

with little effort. Then he turned that side of the box away
from him. At arm's length, he slowly lifted the lid of the box
open. Nothing happened. He peered over the top of the
upright lid and looked down into the box. He saw a thin
leather pouch.

Reaching in, Victor lifted one corner of the dark suede
envelope. He heard a faint cracking sound, like dry leaves,
inside it. Gently lifting the pouch by two corners with his
fingertips, he saw it had a flap on the underside. Carefully
sliding his fingers under the loose flap, he pulled the envelope open and saw several sheets of what appeared to be
parchment pages. He lightly touched their edges to see if
they were brittle. The paper was dry and stiff, but apparently
not disintegrating.

As he slid them from the leather pouch he saw that they
were covered in handwriting—bold, masculine cursive in
thick black ink. Turning the small stack of papers upright, he
realized that he was looking at a letter.

Victor took another deep breath, relaxed again, and
looked all around. He was still alone. Looking down at the top
page of several sheets of paper in his hands, he began to read.

My Dear Friend:

I call you "Dear Friend" for we are of the same cast. If
face-to-face, we would sense this special kinship between
us. You are unique, for you took most unusual steps in an
attempt to find what you hold here. Not knowing what
you would discover—if anything at all—you journeyed
into the unknown. No one told you to make this journey;

you made it of your own accord, listening to the still, small Voice within.

What you seek is here: the elusive Secret men and women through the ages long to discover. It is the Secret your heart yearns for. It is the secret your mind cannot grasp.

I know nothing about your particular circumstances, whether you are young or old, male or female, married or single, religious or not. I do know, however, that you are in search of a better life. How do I know? Because I have known the same personal dissatisfaction and internal conflict you know. Once, I moved fretfully and fearfully from job to job, from city to city, always thinking that the next place would be the "right" place, forever worrying that others would gain the reward before I did. That life was no life. It was, instead, a nightmare of elusive, unfulfilled desires.

But I began to realize, with the help of many mentors—who appeared to me, just as I am now appearing to you, in writing—that there was another way to live.

To enter this new life, however, you must take the first step. Cease worrying about who you were, and who you may someday become. Bury the dead Past, and trust not the Future. *Stay Here.* Rarely will you meet a person who is Here. Most are sadly lost to regrets about the past and fears of the future, lost to the ordinary, anxious thoughts that imperil our existence.

Only By Staying Here Can You Ever Change. When you ask "How?" realize that Now is always the answer to how.

Like you, I sought success; for many years I floundered. Life was a raging battle. I would advance one pace only to retreat two. I frantically contrived for wealth and security. But what I managed to gain became the object of my fears of losing it, and so was soon lost to my own ignorance and greed. Mine was the hellish existence that most never escape. But I, too, was given the Key, the Secret Key I now pass to you that opens the Door of Doors. Behind this Door is all you can imagine, yet much more than you are capable of imagining. Even to try is to sully It.

Your discovery of this Secret places you on the threshold you were born to cross. From this day forward, your life is changed. Discovering this letter, you will forever know that the Door exists. I assure you it does. Entering this Door is what the still, small Voice in you thirsts for and ceaselessly nudges you toward. It knows that all your deeds, dreams, and desires have fallen short. The world may even elevate and envy you, yet the still, small Voice reminds you of the shortfall. It gently stirs and tells you there is Something more you need to find. But here lies the mystery, that timeless paradox: To enter the Door, you must lose yourself. On the other side, you will live from a new perspective, a higher vantage point. From that invisible plateau you will receive perfect instruction by which you will conduct all your affairs.

No longer will doubt, confusion, and fear darken your spirits. Your actions will no longer be mere reactions; you will be purposeful and live from true confidence. You will become invisible to events. The day's headlines will have no affect on you or your choices. Indeed, when you receive instruction issued from behind the Door, there is but one Right Choice to make in every instance, and you will make it without effort, without thinking.

What I am about to reveal to you has been known by only a fortunate few. It obviously is not known by the masses, by educators, or by the so-called learned among us. Precious few have ever heard this revelation, although some who have been blessed with this wisdom have rejected it. They resisted and refused to listen, just as you may be so inclined. So this is your chance. I am ennobled to be the one who brings this Secret to you.

Your mind is not the friend you now believe it to be. It is a mere machine that tosses out thoughts incessantly, mechanically. But you are neither your mind nor its myriad of thoughts and emotions. They cannot open the Door. If they could, they would have done so. To cross the threshold to a new life, you must remove yourself from your own thoughts. This can be done. Permit me to explain what only seems unexplainable.

At any moment, you can be in only one of two places mentally: You either are immersed in your thoughts, or you are separate from them. Incredible an instrument as your mind is, it cannot lift you above what it knows. And you have a Divine Instruction within you to transcend what you know, but the mind simply cannot perform this miracle. You must take the step of faith: *Leave your thoughts behind.*

You, as most do, live from your mind—from thoughts and emotions. This is living on the billiard table or in the rushing river. As active and violent as these places are, they are mesmerizing and hypnotic. Living from thoughts as most do is a form of sleep. To remove yourself from this slumber, simply awaken.

Where are your hands now? Are they relaxed or tense? Do you know the expression on your face? Is your brow furrowed and tight? What is the temperature of the air surrounding you? What is the position of your feet? What supports your body this moment, and how is your weight distributed? This awareness of yourself amid your surroundings is Now. In this attentive state you are separate, watching yourself read the words on this paper, witnessing the thoughts and sensations coursing through you.

Becoming awake lifts you out of the tumultuous waters of doubt, anxiety, worry, fear and anger. Your Attention places you on a bridge *over* the tumbling river. You still see the chaos below, but now you are not part of it. You are transformed into an impartial observer. It is in this attentive state that something higher can communicate with you.

It is impossible to sense Its directions while in the cascading waters. Although It is always present, always reaching out to you, your work is to clear a path to receive Its direction. Do this by becoming awake and attentive. Return to Now.

Rarely will you meet a person who is in the Now state. Most are forever lost in thought. The secret of Now places you at the Door. It is from the Now state that perfect direction can reach you. You cannot hear the Voice's direction while asleep, just as you cannot touch a beam of light; they are of two distinct and different natures. Your inner ears can "hear" only when you are standing upon the doorstep of Now.

My purpose is not to elaborate, but only to reveal this Secret of taking this first step—leaving thought and returning to Now.

Can you do it—can you actually take this step of faith? Your mind is producing doubtful thoughts now, but yes, you can. Think back on your search for this letter: You had to take a step of faith to locate it. This I intended for the very purpose of proving to you the existence of the Door. It also vividly demonstrates how you cannot—must not—trust or believe what your mind "advises." It did not know the location of this letter. Indeed, thoughts shouted at you to give up the search. To locate this hidden letter, you had to leave the certainty of your mind and its thoughts. Now you will work at doing so in greater and greater measure *consciously*, from the attentive, awakened state. You will work from Now.

Be as vigilant as you are able; observe yourself as often as you can remember. Observe the numerous states you enter and exit from each day. Inquire of yourself, "Who is this that is angry? doubtful? fearful? excited? depressed?" *It is not you*; it is only thoughts in your mind *using* you!

When you do this long enough, an entirely new understanding will emerge and you will begin to think in a manner differently than you do presently.

What will happen? You will become a new person! You will see, hear, and sense as never before. The demon fear will retreat and fall away more and more. You will receive directions to proceed that seem impossible. Take that first step—no more, no less—and the next will be revealed. In this way, you will pass through what formerly appeared to be solid brick walls that you avoided. Your

way out is *through* the illusory brick walls! Now you will
seek "the impossible," knowing it is the very doorway out!

Always remember that whatever appears as a solid wall
is a mere illusion created by the rushing river of thought.
It is no more significant than an ant—*disguised* as a brick
wall! The *only* way to banish this illusion is to proceed
through it, watching your fear and trepidation all the
while. In this one way, you will know from yourself that it
is all an illusion.

While you are conducting business, seated at the dining table, enjoying a walk, conversing with
another...even as you doze at night, come back to Now.
(Where are you this moment?) Come back to yourself.
Come back to yourself. A thousand times a day. Work at
this. Keep coming back to yourself, to Now.

As thoughts and feelings attempt to confuse and frus-
trate you, awaken. Watch these demons, and they will
pass. You are viewing from a higher place. Do not jump
back into the river, simply observe from above.

Notice others from your watchful state. They live
immersed in thought, just as you have done to this point
in your life. They are tugged and tousled—at one
moment elated, then sullen, teary, depressed, frightened,
and angry the next. As you begin to observe all these
states your mind pulls you through, you will be amazed.
Return from these thoughts to Now; Now cannot be
bandied about. Your attentive state is solid ground; it is
of a level overlooking the billiard table and rushing river.

Do not struggle to understand the thoughts you
observe; be only watchful of them. Treat them as the
outsiders and intruders they are. Say to yourself, "Oh,

look at that angry thought," etc. Become the uninvolved bystander. An indescribable new life awaits you as you do this.

You are not on as high a level in your employment or business as you secretly know you are capable. Until now, if you desired to rise from this level, you knew only to delve into your thoughts, to refer to your cerebral library for answers. But your library is of the same level as the question you pose. Seeking the higher, you must leave the level you presently occupy. To do so, return to Now. In the past, you knew only to delve into your thoughts for the answers you seek. This process uprooted stored information that is lifeless. You found no answer there and your mind then conjured up projections based on these past dead thoughts. This created fantasies and dreams that only perplexed and agitated you more—a vicious, deceitful cycle. This is all your own mind can provide, however. *It does not know the answer you require.* Now knows. From Now comes the Intelligence that knows you and your every need.

When you know not what to do, return to Now. Now knows. Wait there, and what you need will come to you. What you need is not self-produced.

Of course, there are those who gain the world's esteem and manage to gather its riches, but you will find that it sooner or later destroys them. They gained it out of persistence and the Law of Accident. Most everyone who persists does acquire, but of what value is it if it destroys? There is nothing wrong in gaining worldly treasures if you have first the higher wisdom. See for yourself; observe the world's business and political leaders. They are like an infant happening upon a shimmering object; the glow and glisten entices the child to handle it, to play with it. Little does the infant know the bright shining plaything is a finely polished knife. But with understanding, the knife is a keen tool, very practical and productive in wise, skilled hands.

Turn instead to your only true friend—Now. As a child turns to a parent, simply ask for direction. Have no ideas, schemes, or plans. Simply ask—*knowing that you do not know*—and then await the Answer.

Have no preconceived notions; do not attempt to identify or describe any outcome. What a relief it is to know that you are not responsible for (nor capable of) generating right answers! That is the same as attempting to instruct a tree how to form and develop. The seed does not require directions from you; it already contains a Divine Instruction—just as do you. You do not know the outcome, you do not know how. But Now knows; Now is how.

Intelligence knows you completely; It is your one true friend. It knows what is highest and best for you. Your mind—intellect—does not know. So cease your continual turning to your thoughts for answers; they have none above the level you are on. If they did, would you still be on your search? If thought held the answers you require, you would not be questioning.

I can relate countless stories of true revelations and miracles that came to me through the Door. They were grander than I could have imagined or dared to request! Merely take the first step—honestly and innocently ask.

Then confidently await the Right Answer that has been attempting to contact you all along!

Notice—right now—how your mind is clamoring. It is telling you, "This is wrong," "How could this be so?," "What nonsense!" Your mind does not favor being the target of this bright light you are shining upon it. If you believe what your mind shouts, you will continue on as you have; you will be just one more of the mass of lemmings—running blindly; asleep—to their impending doom.

But you are different; you sense that the still, small Voice attempts to lead you to something greater than yourself, and thus the solution to every problem and limitation. Give Now this chance and see for yourself. Whatever question you have, put it to Now. Now is the way.

My essential directions contained in this letter place you at the gateway to your own revelations; however, you must experience It for yourself. Every question you have, or ever will have, is answered by Now. I shall prepare you and reveal some experiences you are about to undergo as you begin this, the one true journey:

You will find yourself speaking less as you begin observing more and more. Most believe that activity evidences productivity, yet you will begin to see through this fallacy. When idle, your thoughts will protest: "You are wasting time!," "Get to work!," "Idleness means missed opportunities!," "Activity is productivity!," and so on and so on. These are mere tricks of your mind. Watch them as you wait for true Answers to come through the Door. You cannot hear them amid chaos and confusion—the "normal" state of the mind.

I smile in anticipation of your revelations, of your coming awake, truly alive. Revelations await you. Some will unnerve you, others will stupefy your senses. These miraculous events will be evidence that you are transcending this notional world and living from the Higher.

Take the first step: Come back to Now. The next step will be revealed. All that you need to know—and precisely when—is in Now. Nothing is coincidental from Now where chance does not exist. What sleeping people call coincidences and miracles are understood—and commonplace!—from Now.

Be attentive; come back to Now. All—everything!—is there. All true Answers come from Now. Now knows. Take the first step—no more, no less—and the next will be revealed. Do this now.

Good-bye, my Dear Friend.

C. W.

August 1899

P.S. Before replacing this letter, inscribe the initials of your name below.

T.L.	M.F.	H.F.	D.R.	O.S.M.
J.W.T.	N.V.P.	J.C.P.	H.G.	S.B.
T.C.D.	A.E.E.	A.C.	A.G.B.	A.S.
W.C.S.	F.W.W.			

Victor's hands were trembling. Clement Watt knew. Discovering this letter was no accident, and it definitely was not of Victor's doing. Clement Watt had passed his rare understanding—this Gift of gifts—through time and space, even beyond the grave, and placed it in Victor's hands. A calm came over him such as he had never felt. He understood more than ever what Minnie had taught him of the Secret and what she had conveyed about C. W. He thought of the blue rose.

Victor looked down at the fragile pages he held. A thought told him this was all an accident, that he wasn't meant to be the recipient of such a precious message, of the powerful secret he now held. Of course this was a ridiculous thought and he experienced a deep sense of gratitude that he knew it now. Until yesterday, when he met Minnie, he would have believed that thought, bought it hook, line, and sinker, and suffered the consequences.

Thank God for Clement Watt.

Victor tucked the pages back into the leather pouch and replaced it in the wooden box. Before closing and locking the secret compartment door, he felt inside the hidden attic to be sure nothing else was concealed there. It was empty. Victor closed and locked the door, removed the key, and placed it in his pocket.

Picking up his small wooden treasure box, he departed for the library at the end of Park Street.

The same pretty young woman who directed him to the *Daily Gazette* two days earlier was working behind the librarian's counter when he entered. She looked up, recognized him, and smiled hello. Victor returned the silent greeting.

"Hello," he said. "I'm back again, this time to use your copy machine."

"It's right back there. You'll need dimes to make copies. Did you find that old newspaper you were looking for?"

"Yes, yes I did." Victor said. "Mr. Jessup, the owner, was very helpful. They've made microfiche copies of all their editions going back to about 1890."

"Good. I'm glad you found what you were looking for."

Victor asked for change to use the copy machine and then remembered the poem.

"Oh, do you have a collection of Longfellow poetry you can direct me to?"

"Yes, we have several. Are you looking for a particular work?"

"Yes, I am: A *Psalm of Life*."

"Umm, I don't remember that one. You go get started on your copying and I'll find it for you. A *Psalm of Life*...."

"That would be great. Thanks."

Victor carried the precious wooden box back to a table near the copy machine, placed it on the table and sat down. Carefully opening it, he reached in, opened the leather pouch, and removed the parchment papers.

The same calm he felt when he first discovered C. W.'s message back at the well enveloped him. The answer to all his prayers, supplications, yearnings, and desires was here in front of him. A scripture came to mind: Ask, and it shall be given to you; seek, and you shall find; knock, and it shall be opened to you. Recalling the past three days' events, Victor thought that this was the exact manner in which they all unfolded.

He slowly read the parchment again. It all is so simple, he thought. But it's completely different from all the authors and lectures he had read and heard before. They were nothing like what C. W. revealed in these few words.

In just these past two days, since meeting Minnie, I see how very little I understand the thoughts in my own mind. I see how little I'm even aware of them! I see that I'm at their mercy, and that most of them are definitely not operating in my best interest! These thoughts in my head make a terrible master, and that's exactly what I am—their slave! I can't stop them, I can't alter them, but just like a thunderstorm, I don't have to be battered and blown about by them. What a different way to live!

"Here it is, A *Psalm of Life*. What a beautiful poem. I'm so glad you asked for it." The young librarian placed a very old, thick book down on the table next to Victor. She never commented on what Victor considered to be an odd-looking collection in front of him—the old box, leather pouch, and parchment pages. He looked up and thanked her.

The old book was a collection of Longfellow writings, opened to the poem he had been looking for.

A Psalm of Life
What the Young Man Said to the Psalmist

Tell me not, in mournful numbers,
Life is but an empty dream!—
For the soul is dead that slumbers,
And things are not what they seem.

Life is real! Life is earnest!

And the grave is not its goal;
Dust thou art, to dust returnest,
Was not spoken of the soul.

Not enjoyment, and not sorrow,
Is our destined end or way;
But to act, that each to-morrow
Find us farther than to-day.

Art is long, and Time is fleeting,
And our hearts, though stout and brave,
Still, like muffled drums, are beating
Funeral marches to the grave.

In the world's broad field of battle,
In the bivouac of Life,
Be not like dumb, driven cattle!
Be a hero in the strife!

Trust no Future, howe'er pleasant!
Let the dead Past bury its dead!
Act,—act in the living Present!
Heart within, and God o'erhead!

Lives of great men all remind us
We can make our lives sublime,
And, departing, leave behind us
Footprints on the sands of time;

Footprints that perhaps another,
Sailing o'er life's solemn main,
A forlorn and shipwrecked brother,
Seeing, shall take heart again.

Let us, then, be up and doing,
With a heart for any fate;
Still achieving, still pursuing,
Learn to labor and to wait.

It's all right here, on this single page. Longfellow said it all in this one poem, but I never would have really known what he was talking about without Minnie and Clement.

"And, departing, leave behind us
Footprints on the sands of time...."
This poem is all about C. W.'s life.

Victor looked down at C. W.'s signature and a sense of wonder welled up in him. Then he looked at the initials that had been added. All these people had also discovered these very pages that Victor was reading now. *I wonder who they were, or are? I wonder how they came to discover the well? The same way I did? Or did C. W. leave other clues that also lead to it? I wonder how these people's lives have changed, and have they, too, left footprints on the sand?*

With a ballpoint pen, Victor added his own initials to the parchment.

Victor thanked the librarian, carefully gathered his treasure, and meandered back across town to the Children's Home. He had much to think about, and his mind was working furiously with that day's events.

He remembered Longfellow's words and understood them better now: Trust no future, howe'er pleasant!

Constant vigilance, that's the secret. The mind will take any-thing—past or future—and dwell upon it, project from it, and cre-ate emotions—good and bad—around it. It will do anything to avoid the present, the Now.

People live their lives within these past and future thoughts, completely missing Now! That's why C. W. said Now is how.

Victor carefully and precisely tucked the wooden box and its contents up into the little attic space in the well's roof and locked the compartment door. He wondered when—and by whom—it would be opened again, if ever. He then returned the key to Mr. McCully, who was as cordial as before, and asked no questions of him.

With ample time remaining before the last van back to the Grand Hotel, Victor continued along First Avenue and past Main Street, down toward the river.

Named River Street, it really wasn't a street at all—it was a large, wide boardwalk, for pedestrians only.

Expansive lush green lawns rose to thick, color-filled flower beds surrounding the oversized two- and three-story wood-framed homes on River Street. Wrought iron garden lights shaped like small bells lined stone and brick walkways that led up to each home's spacious screened porch where their owners would sit in the evening. Victor imagined them sipping drinks and gazing upon the river below. Nearly every home was enclosed within the expansive, reaching branches of magnifi-cent giant-leafed magnolias and moss-shrouded oaks.

On the opposite side of the boardwalk were grassy knolls gently sloping down to the quiet, slow-moving river. There, at a well-weathered dock, sat the *Coincidental*.

As old as she was, only the absence of modern plastic, fiberglass, and neon colors suggested her age. She, truly, was shipshape, sitting stout and handsome in the water.

An obvious name for her would have been the *River Queen*, but then again, her owner was Clement Watt, a man who understood this world. He was not swayed by its useless, erroneous concerns with prestige, power, and image. *Coincidental* was obviously too casual a name for this yacht. And that's the very reason why C. W. must have christened her so.

Victor sat on the edge of the boardwalk and re-read his copies of the parchment. Looking up at the *Coincidental*, he whispered, "Thank you, Mr. Watt."

According to the stately old clock at Main Street and First Avenue, Victor was fifteen minutes early. He walked the remaining block down Main Street to the oak in the cul-de-sac where the hotel van delivered and picked up its passengers.

Victor was reading C. W.'s message as the van turned the circle and came to a stop. As he looked up, Christine was running toward him, her smile and eyes shining.

"I just missed you too much, so I came to find you!" She hugged and kissed him.

"It's all over now, hon. I found even more than we could have dreamed of."

With an arm around each other they boarded the van and began the trip back to the hotel. Victor pointed out the *Coincidental* as the van clattered through the old covered bridge out of town.

CHAPTER 12

The manager of the Grand Hotel hosted a farewell breakfast the morning the group departed. As he offered up a toast, he concluded it saying, "I trust your visit here with us has been relaxing and rewarding."

That's when Christine looked up at Victor, as they both silently spoke C. W.'s name.

Ever since the van ride together, back from Victor's final momentous day in town, they had been discussing their new-found secret and broadening understanding. They were like two children sharing new toys and discoveries as insights from their new, growing awareness would come to them. Victor realized more than ever what a rare gift he had in Christine, that she, too, knew the still, small Voice and understood and cherished Minnie's and C. W.'s priceless words. Victor felt very fortunate indeed.

The cool, dry air in the jet was a welcome change from the heavy mugginess outside. But the thick, rich greenbelts and fields below, all dotted and separated by ponds, lakes, rivers, and streams, were a sight he would miss as they approached the rugged, dry southwest.

Victor opened the *Daily Gazette* he had picked up in the lobby of the Grand Hotel that morning before they departed. He noticed it was three days old and wondered how it managed to survive so long on the coffee table he found it on.

As he turned to page two, the article's headline jumped out at him:

Minnie Nelson Leaves Us at 83

"She was singing, even whistling a little," said her daughter Colleen, 50, "when she went to her room for her afternoon nap yesterday. She had just had a meeting with a very promising young man and was unusually impressed with his desire to learn."

She fell asleep reading *Something You Should Know,* a small book by Clement Watt, her lifelong friend, teacher, and the benefactor of the town's Children's Home.

And so, peacefully ended the rather amazing life of one of our most beloved, yet little-known citizens. The eldest daughter of W. J. and Emma Ward, Minnie Nelson was an unofficial advisor and confidante to celebrities, politicians, and industrialists, many of whom have been spotted sitting with her on the famous front porch of Emma's boarding house. Mr. Lee Iacocca of Ford and Chrysler fame was reportedly seen there recently.

The family plans a private memorial service and requests no flowers.

Victor handed Christine the newspaper and pointed to the small article. He leaned back in his seat, looked out the small oval window at the clear, pure, blue sky and thought of the rose. He closed his eyes and thought of Minnie and what she had shared and taught him in, literally, the very last moments of her life. Then he considered the probability of all the events of the past week ever happening, right down to picking up this three-day-old newspaper in the lobby of a busy, immaculately kept hotel.

All of a sudden, Christine became animated. Victor heard the newspaper rustling.

"Victor! This is, this is just..."

"Coincidental?" he whispered with a smile. "Better get used to it."

Victor squeezed her hand.

*L*ives of great men all remind us
We can make our lives sublime,
And, departing, leave behind us
Footprints on the sands of time;

*F*ootprints that perhaps another,
Sailing o'er life's solemn main,
A forlorn and shipwrecked brother,
Seeing, shall take heart again.

*L*et each one examine his thoughts, and he will
find them all occupied with the past and the future.
We scarcely ever think of the present, and if we think
of it, it is only to take light from it to arrange the
future.... So we never live, but we hope to live; and,
as we are always preparing to be happy, it is inevitable
we should never be so.

Pascal

*C*onfine yourself to the present.

Aurelius

On the following page you will find listed, with their current prices, some of the books now available on related subjects. Your book dealer stocks most of these and will stock new titles in the Llewellyn series as they become available. We urge your patronage.

TO GET A FREE CATALOG

You are invited to write for our bi-monthly news magazine/catalog, *Llewellyn's New Worlds of Mind and Spirit*. A sample copy is free, and it will continue coming to you at no cost as long as you are an active mail customer. Or you may subscribe for just $10 in the United States and Canada ($20 overseas, first class mail). Many bookstores also have *New Worlds* available to their customers. Ask for it.

In *New Worlds* you will find news and features about new books, tapes and services; announcements of meetings and seminars; helpful articles; author interviews and much more. Write to:

Llewellyn's New Worlds of Mind and Spirit
P.O. Box 64383-K580, St. Paul, MN 55164-0383, U.S.A.

TO ORDER BOOKS AND TAPES

If your book store does not carry the titles described on the following pages, you may order them directly from Llewellyn by sending the full price in U.S. funds, plus postage and handling (see below).

Credit card orders: VISA, MasterCard, American Express are accepted. Call us toll-free within the United States and Canada at 1-800-THE-MOON.

Special Group Discount: Because there is a great deal of interest in group discussion and study of the subject matter of this book, we offer a 20% quantity discount to group leaders or agents. Our Special Quantity Price for a minimum order of five copies of *A Rich Man's Secret* is $40.00 cash-with-order. Include postage and handling charges noted below.

Postage and Handling: Include $4 postage and handling for orders $15 and under; $5 for orders *over* $15. There are no postage and handling charges for orders over $100. Postage and handling rates are subject to change. We ship UPS whenever possible within the continental United States; delivery is guaranteed. Please provide your street address as UPS does not deliver to P.O. boxes. Orders shipped to Alaska, Hawaii, Canada, Mexico and Puerto Rico will be sent via first class mail. Allow 4-6 weeks for delivery.

International orders: Airmail – add retail price of each book and $5 for each non-book item (audiotapes, etc.); Surface mail – add $1 per item.

Minnesota residents add 7% sales tax.

Mail orders to:
Llewellyn Worldwide
P.O. Box 64383-K580
St. Paul, MN 55164-0383, U.S.A.
For customer service, call (612) 291-1970.

THE SECRET OF LETTING GO
Guy Finley

Whether you need to let go of a heartache, a habit, a worry or a discontent, *The Secret of Letting Go* shows you how to call upon your hidden powers and how they can take you through and beyond any challenge or problem. This book reveals the secret source of a brand-new kind of inner strength. With a foreword by Desi Arnaz Jr., and introduction by Dr. Jesse Freeland, *The Secret of Letting Go* is a pleasing balance of questions and answers, illustrative examples, truth tales, and stimulating dialogues that allow the reader to share in the exciting discoveries that lead up to lasting self-liberation.

This is a book for the discriminating, intelligent, and sensitive reader who is looking for *real* answers.

0-87542-223-3, 240 pgs. 5¼ x 8   **$9.95**

FREEDOM FROM THE TIES THAT BIND
The Secret of Self Liberation
Guy Finley

Imagine how your life would flow *without* the weight of those weary inner voices constantly convincing you that "you can't," or complaining that someone else should be blamed for the way *you* feel. The weight of the world on your shoulders would be replaced by a bright, new sense of freedom. *You could choose to live the way* YOU *want.* In *Freedom from the Ties that Bind*, Guy Finley reveals hundreds of Celestial, but down-to-earth, secrets of Self-Liberation that show exactly how to be fully independent, and *free of any condition not to your liking*. Even difficult people won't be able to turn your head or test your temper. Enjoy meaningful relationships founded *in conscious choice—not through self-defeating compromise*. Learn the secrets of unlocking the door to your own Free Mind. Be empowered to break free of any self-punishing pattern, and make the discovery that who you really are is already everything you've ever wanted to be.

0-87542-217-9, 240 pgs., 6 x 9   **$10.00**

DESIGNING YOUR OWN DESTINY
The Power to Shape Your Future
Guy Finley

This book is for those who are ready for a book on self-transformation with principles that actually *work*. *Designing Your Own Destiny* is a practical, powerful guide that tells you, in plain language, exactly what you need to do to fundamentally change yourself and your life for the better, permanently.

After reading *Designing Your Own Destiny*, you'll understand why you are perfectly equal to every task you set for yourself, and that you truly *can* change your life for the better!

1-56718-278-X, 160 pgs., mass market   **$6.99**